Ninth Ward Blues

by

Janelle Smith Toussant

This book is a work of fiction. Names, characters and incidents are the product of the author's imagination. Any resemblance to actual events or persons is entirely coincidental and beyond the intent of the author.

indie girl publishing

P.O. Box 1572
Fresno, Texas 77545

Prologue

Music has always been a part of my life. As a matter of fact, mama likes to say that as soon as she placed me in my crib I started moaning and humming, sound like I was trying to sing a lullaby to myself.

All the highlights and the lowlights of my life; hell, even all the lights that fall in between, seem to be linked in my brain to either one song or another. First kiss: New Edition's Lost in Love. First Dance: Wham's Careless Whispers. First broken heart: Sade's Is It a Crime. It's funny how you can hear only a few cords from a song and it'll transport you back in time to a particular person or place.

I've been singing for as long as I can remember; and I sound pretty good too, if I do say so myself. I'll never forget my first solo performance. I was four years old and I sang 'His Eye is on the Sparrow' at Mount Zion Baptist Church. Even at such a young age, I was hooping so hard that Sister Francis stood up out of her seat, caught the Holy Ghost, and almost lost her pageboy wig before I even got to the chorus.

Come to think of it, the only time that my grandmother, Ma-Me, seemed to be pleased with me is when I was singing in church, giving my all at the altar.

I remember once saying that my existence was one long song. And every funny story and every sad occurrence were the verses that make up the rhythm and the blues of my life. I thought that I was so clever coming up with that line. I thought that I had my life all mapped out. I would become a rich and famous singer and dazzle my audience with unmatched vocals and lyrics written to break hearts.

But now I realize that I didn't know shit. And sometimes the crying doesn't stop when the music ends.

Part One

Verse one: back down memory lane

Ma-Me lived in the raggediest house in the Ninth Ward. And that's saying a lot, considering her house was smack dab in the middle of a block *full* of ugly, raggedy houses. People walking past would often stop in their tracks and stare at the oddly shaped, gray monstrosity. Perched atop eighteen cinderblock stairs, it seemed to loom down at you, threatening, like a haunted house in some children's story come to life. Yet, at the same time it seemed almost regal; reigning supreme over the ward and all its happenings.

We started spending summers at Ma-Me's right around my thirteenth birthday. Mama and daddy decided they were tired of the constant fussing and fighting, so daddy left and moved into a small apartment across town. Mama shipped my little sister and me off to the Ninth Ward, to Ma-Me's run-down shotgun house while she took some time to *get herself together.*

I can still remember the look on my parents faces as they gave us the news. Daddy was home early from his job as a construction foreman. He had a look of guilt and unease on his face that immediately let me know that whatever his announcement was it would not be something I wanted to hear.

Mama sat on the couch next to him. They were side by side as if they were both on the same page, but I could tell by the way her arms were folded and by the way her lips were stretched into a thin line, she was holding back what she really wanted to say.

"Have a seat, Tracey," daddy instructed me as I walked through the door. The cadence of his voice was lower than I'd ever heard it before and there was no trace of his trademark smile anywhere on his face.

"Your mama and I want to talk to you and your sister," he said and took a gulp of the Miller Lite that he held.

I plopped down onto the green chenille loveseat, annoyed that this impromptu family meeting was cutting into my Cosby Show time, but mostly scared that what they were going to say would change my life.

That's when I noticed my sister, Lynette, for the first time. She sat so still and quiet that she seemed to blend in with the furniture. I realized at that moment just how wrong everything was. Lynette was never still, and she was never quiet.

To call me a daddy's girl would probably be the understatement of the year. I know that the saying goes "mama's baby, daddy's maybe", but there was no denying that I was David Dubois's daughter.

We didn't look much alike; Lynette had daddy's caramel colored complexion and coarse brown hair; whereas, people would often look at me, with my copper skin and heart shaped face and say, "Tracey girl, Diane just spit you out, didn't she?"

Despite the lack of resemblance, daddy and I had the same personalities. We both loved to sing, laugh, and felt that 'Thou Shalt not fail to dream' should have been the eleventh commandment.

I guess that's part of the reason mama and I seemed to clash often following their divorce. The rational part of me knew that it took two people to break up a marriage, but the emotional part of me couldn't help thinking that if mama was just a little more easy going or more understanding, or just *more*, daddy would still be around.

I was also ticked off at the amount of time that we had to spend in the Ninth Ward, at Ma-Me's house. Mama explained to us that she needed to go back to school in order to make more money since she wasn't getting a dime from daddy, but that didn't mean that I had to like our new living arrangements. Besides the fact that Ma-Me's house was a broken-down shoebox, which was bad enough, Ma-Me wasn't the easiest person in the world to get along with. She was one of the grouchiest people that I've ever met. And I swear, for the life of me, I couldn't think of a time when she just threw her head back and simply laughed out loud.

I'm not saying that I didn't love my grandmother, because I did. I loved her to death. I loved the way she pulled me between her legs, greased my scalp and plaited my hair. I loved the way she

5

whipped out the Robitussin whenever Lynette or I so much as coughed or hiccupped. And I loved the way she was so dedicated to her church that she would place her last wrinkled dollar into the building fund basket.

So yeah, I loved Ma-Me, but she made it very difficult to like her at times. She had her ways, and they were funny. She also practiced favoritism, and I wasn't her favorite. I'll just leave it at that.

Verse two: It's so hard to say goodbye to yesterday

As much as the disappearance of daddy from our lives devastated us, we were even more upset by our apparent abandonment by mama. She made a deal with us, that we would spend weekdays by Ma-Me's during the summer while she worked and went to school; but on Friday evenings, immediately after punching out, she would pick us up and take us home to spend the weekend with her.

Every Friday night promptly at five o'clock we would sit at the top of those stone steps in front of Ma-Me's house, mosquitoes tearing us up, and wait for her. Sometimes we'd sit there for hours. Sometimes we'd sit there all night. We'd count the cars to help the time go by. Five more cars and it'll be mama...ten more cars and it'll be mama.

One Friday night, towards the end of the summer, we were so excited about going home that we began our vigil at 4:30. Our next door neighbor, and my best friend, Valarie, was having a birthday party and I wanted to make sure that I got home in time to get her a birthday present.

Five o'clock came and went. We must have counted over a hundred cars and still no mama. Finally, I called home.

"Mama, why haven't you come to pick us up?" I whined when she answered the phone.

"I'm on my way," she promised and hung up before I was able to utter another word.

Another hundred cars passed and still no mama. I tried calling her back but this time there was no answer.

I called Valarie.

"Yeah, her car is right outside y'all house," she seemed to take pleasure in reporting.

Lynette and I took turns all night calling her back. Instead of counting cars this time we counted rings. Thirty, forty, fifty...she never picked up.

Eventually Lynette and I fell asleep, curled up in each other's arms.

Verse three: Jesus is love

Lynette and I sat in the choir stand at New Hope Baptist Church, freezing our butts off underneath our lavender choir robes and pretending that we weren't watching the door, waiting for mama. We were on program to sing a duet for the pastor's anniversary and mama promised that she'd be there.

Church has always been a part of our lives, and even though our family was going through transition, you could still find us together on Sunday morning, praising the Lord.

Try as I might, I can't think of a time when I was not learning about the Resurrection in Sunday School or singing about Jesus' love for the little children, in the youth choir. It always trips me out when I hear people say that they were too tired to get up to go to church. That was simply unheard of in my house. It's not like we were overly Christian. You know—the types that eat, drink and breathe "The Lord"—but you'd better believe that we were not fixin' to open our mouths to tell Ma-Me we were *too tired* to go to church!

I can hear her now, going on and on, huffing and puffing and gritting her teeth indignantly at the gull of us for opening our mouths and uttering something so stupid and trifling.

"Are you too tired to play? Are you too tired to eat? Are you too tired to go outside and get that switch, so I can beat your behind black and blue?"

We were more than halfway through the service and still no sign of mama. I could tell that her absence was weighing heavy on Lynette's mind by the way that her bottom lip was slightly poked out. I was about to start pouting myself, but then I saw mama tiptoe through the door and slide into the pew next to Ma-Me. Just in time for our performance.

Sister Baptiste began playing the intro and Lynette and I walked to the front of the stage and took the mics. I cleared my throat and pushed the butterflies down.

"Why should I feel discouraged," I began, my high alto floating out of my body like a spirit, "and why should the shadows come."

"Why should my heart feel lonely," Lynette joined in, her soprano voice coming in smooth and strong, "and long for heaven and home."

"*Sing that song, girls!*" Mama stood up and shouted. Ma-Me sat tall with tears of pride glistening in her eyes.

Lynette grabbed my hand and we sang with everything that we had inside of us.

"When Jesus is my portion. A constant friend is he. His eye is on the sparrow and I know he watches me."

The worst part about going to church with Ma-Me was that it took her all day to leave the sanctuary after Sunday morning services. As usual, I waited around, tapping my feet and darn near losing my mind, while she complained to Sister Baptiste about everything from her gall stones to the rising cost of Community Coffee.

The organist snuck a peek at her watch and glanced toward the front vestibule, which gave me hope that we would finally be able to make our escape and I would be able to go home and hang out with Valarie, whose Catholic Church services never lasted more than an hour. Then I spotted mama and Lynette walking towards us. Mama was smiling wide and talking to a tall, big-boned lady, in a faded red dress. Lynette was next to a pudgy, chestnut colored boy in a tight three-piece suit.

I rolled my eyes and thought, *We're never going to get out of here.*

"This is Mrs. Adams and her son, Gregory," mama announced when she approached us. Mama motioned towards Ma-Me. "Mrs. Adams, this is my mother, Mary Elise Douglas."

Mrs. Adams stepped forward, grabbed Ma-Me's hand, and gave it three hard pumps. I snickered to

11

myself because I knew that move would tick Ma-Me off. She hated being touched by strangers. Mama called her the OCD Queen because of the way she always went around cleaning after everybody and washing her hands every five minutes.

"Good afta'noon," Ma-Me muttered, while not so subtly wiping her hands on her rose-colored floral dress.

She eyeballed Mrs. Adams from heel to head, taking in her runny stockings and hand me down dress. Ma-Me believed that a lady should look her best, especially at church. What Me-Me failed to realize was that maybe that dress *was* that lady's best. I was holding my breath, hoping that Ma-Me wouldn't say anything to embarrass us.

"Tracey," mama continued, trying to divert attention from Ma-Me and her rudeness, "Greg just enrolled at McDonogh 35. He might be in your class."

"That's great," I said with a fake smile plastered on my face.

Greg stood there with a thousand-watt smile. After a few uncomfortable minutes, I was beginning to think that maybe something was wrong with the boy, but then he finally spoke.

"That song..." he paused as if he was trying to gather his thoughts. I guess he gave up, because all he came up with is, "...man, that was some song."

"Thanks," I mumbled, trying to avoid making eye contact with him.

I didn't want to be impolite because mama was standing there watching me, and I knew that I would hear her mouth for a month worth of Sundays if I was downright rude, but I wasn't trying to give him any encouragement. Especially, since he was standing there grinning like a fool, looking at me like he was starving, and I was the last biscuit left on the plate.

Verse four: dreamin'

By the time I stepped foot into high school things began to stabilize for our fractured family. We helped Ma-Me board up her dump in the Ninth Ward and she moved in with us in New Orleans East, but we hadn't seen hide nor hair of daddy in better than three years. We'd gone from having someone that was completely ingrained in our lives and our everyday existence, to having a father that we never saw anymore.

When they first separated, he would pick us up most weekends and take us out for ice cream and pizza. But it wasn't long before one missed weekend turned into a month, and then before I knew it, I had to think hard to remember the feel of his goodnight kiss or the sound of his laugh.

And as for Mama, she did a one hundred-eighty degree turn and went from being an absentee mom to being all up in my business. It felt like every time I turned around, she was there in my face telling me what to do and where I could and could not go.

It seemed like she'd gotten it into her head that Lynette and I were all she had left, so she was doing everything she could to hold on to us.

She almost had me wishing for those days when her grip was as loose as a cheap weave.

"So, mama, have you had a chance to think about it yet?" I asked as I rummaged through the brown paper bags that covered nearly every vacant spot in the kitchen.

There was absolutely nothing like *grocery making* day. When we walked through the door with armloads of Winn-Dixie bags, you'd think that we'd won the lottery, with all the noise and commotion that Lynette and I made.

"Tracey, I asked you to put the food up, not make an even bigger mess than before."

"Sorry, ma," I said, continuing my quest for the Cap 'n Crunch. "So, have you considered it?" I asked again and then added, as if she needed any further clarification, "...about me joining the singing group?"

I was referring to a flyer that I'd seen on a bulletin board at the grocery store. There wasn't much information given, it simply read:

GIRL SINGER NEEDED FOR R & B GROUP.
ONLY THE SERIOUS SHOULD APPLY.
(504) 949-4122

I knew as soon as I saw it that that flyer was left there just for me.

"Tracey, I told you in the store, I told you in the car, and now I am telling you in this kitchen...the answer is no! I'm not about to let a daughter of mine go around singing with some group that I don't even know anything about." It was clear she'd had about enough of this conversation. "You're just going to have to be satisfied singing in the church choir," she added as if that was some kind of great consolation.

I rolled my eyes behind her back. I knew before even asking her what her stance would be. Mama always acted like she was resentful of daddy's talent and the amount of time that he spent chasing his dream of being a singer, and now she was acting the same with me.

She is such a hypocrite, I thought.

Mama finally graduated college so she was embarking on a new career as a pediatric nurse. She'd even started dating a man named, Lester Jones, who had attended our church. It seemed like she was ready to put herself out there and go for the things that she wanted, so who was she to tell me that I couldn't do the same.

I decided to give up on the conversation, but I wasn't giving up on the dream.

Verse five: everyday, I have the blues

The air was heavy with the smell of freshly cut grass and the funk of wannabe teenaged athletes; it was a one-two punch that assaulted my sinuses. I was practicing my cheer without much enthusiasm, trying to shake off a bad headache and an equally bad attitude. I was teed-off because we had just finished tryouts for squad captain, and Valarie was awarded the top spot. That was such bull! Everybody knew that the only reason Coach Warren made her team captain was because Valerie was cute and had good hair. The fact that Val was always kissing up to her, bucking her up with compliments on her pieced together outfits or her three-year-old, played out haircut didn't seem to hurt matters either.

Valarie Boudreaux was my best friend in the entire world, even though we had about as much in common as Kool-Aid and coffee.

I glanced over at her and watched as she flashed a wide smile and shook what the good Lord gave her. I rolled my eyes. I was surprised at the resentment that I felt and tried, unsuccessfully, to put my emotions in check.

For as long as I've known Valerie, things always seemed to come so easily for her. Whatever, or whoever, she wanted, Valarie got. From the cutest boy in school to the nicest new kicks, once Val set her sights on them, they were hers.

Normally, it didn't bother me, especially since our taste in most things was so different. Besides, I had long since learned to shrug off Valarie's antics as just Val being Val. But there were times like this when her antics annoyed me. Val had no interest in being captain. She tried out and accepted the position simply because she knew that she could. I couldn't help but wonder just who my best friend was. It also made me speculate about myself, questioning why I continued to let her get away with it all.

I turned the notion of jealousy over in my mind, but quickly batted it away. I was not jealous of Valarie. She was clearly the more attractive of the two of us, often being referred to as "beautiful" while I was called "cute", but I was okay with that. I knew that with my singing talent there were times when Val was jealous of me, though she would never admit it.

Later that night, Val rushed through my door so fast I had to check to see if the police was behind her.

"What in the world is going on?" I asked as she slapped a folded newspaper onto my unmade bed.

Val's long black hair was tied into a messy side ponytail and she was wearing mismatched wrinkled sweats. She looked nothing like the *put together* Val that I was used to seeing.

Whereas I normally went with a more natural look—blue jeans, tee shirts and tied back hair, Val hardly ever stepped out of her door without looking as clean as the Board of Health. I knew that whatever got her out of her house looking less than her best had to be important, at least to her.

"Val, what is it?" I asked again, even though I knew that she wouldn't answer me right away.

Val intended to squeeze every drop of drama out of the moment. She smirked at me and finally answered, "Check out who's featured on the society page."

I picked the paper up and saw my father's face looking back at me. Daddy's group, Ninth Ward Blues, was the opening act at the Zulu Ball. The picture was grainy and the article was short, but still, my heart jumped in my chest when I saw it.

I shrugged my shoulders and scrunched up my mouth, acting like it was no big deal, but I couldn't wait for Valarie to leave. I needed to be alone so that I could sort through my feelings. Of course, she didn't pick up on my mood.

"The gall him, having the nerve to be skinning and grinning for the camera when he can't even be bothered to come and see his own kids," Val said.

I didn't respond, but deep down I agreed with her. Still, I didn't like her saying it.

That night, I had a dream about daddy. He needed a female lead for his group and he called and asked me to come and audition for him. He called me!

He pulled in front of the house in the same beat up red pickup truck that he drove away in, and held me so tight that I thought that he would never let go. We drove to the studio and daddy started bragging to all his friends that his daughter was the best singer in the city. I stepped up the mic to prove his big talk true, but when I opened my mouth to sing, nothing came out. Nothing at all. Daddy glared at me and told me that I was no daughter of his. Then he turned away and left me standing there with the mic in my hand.

Verse six: little child running wild

I woke up the next morning like a young woman on a mission. I didn't care what mama said, I was trying out for the singing group. Daddy was following his dreams and I was going to do the same.

It didn't take much for me to get Val to skip school with me. We scraped together what little money we had, paid Lynette five dollars to keep her mouth shut, and used the rest to catch the bus and then rode the St. Charles streetcar to the address that was given to me when I called the number on the flyer.

The name of the group was L9, which confused me to no end since there were only three girls in the group—four if you included me.

L9 was an acronym for Lower Nine, or more precisely, the Lower Ninth Ward of New Orleans; one of the hardest, most ghetto parts of the city. Despite its dumb name, I had a good feeling about L9. Lord, those girls could sing! Ebony and Essence, the twins, were twenty and had just graduated from Joseph S. Clark High School—two years later than scheduled. They were so proud of their accomplishment that they mentioned it at least three times within the first twenty minutes of meeting them.

They were identical; tall, almost 5'10", with medium brown skin and small, slanted eyes that twinkled underneath black, bushy eyebrows.

Patrice was nineteen. She too was a graduate of Clark. She was petite, 5'2", about 100 pounds soaking wet, and as cute as she could be with her café au lait complexion, little button nose, and dimples as deep as the pot holes in front of her grandmother's house, where we rehearsed.

At seventeen, I was the baby of the group.

I was scared to death when we arrived. The twins opened the door and stared at us like they were trying to decide whether to let us in or tear the door off its hinges and beat us down with it.

I was about to turn around and run away, but then, like a pair of synchronized swimmers, they smiled and said, "Come on in here and show us what y'all got."

I assumed I was in because what was supposed to be a twenty-minute audition turned into a jam session that lasted over two hours. After that, I was handed a stack of songs and was instructed to have them memorized for the next practice.

22

My life became a never-ending cycle of school, church, and L9. Mama had no idea that I joined the group, so I had to get creative with coming up with excuses to get out of the house. I would love to say I felt guilty about being dishonest to her, but that would be telling another lie. I loved singing with the girls. If it meant getting a beat down from mama if she ever found out, then those were licks I would have to take.

To make matters worse, Valarie had been acting funny lately. I knew it was because the girls from L9 practically laughed in her face when she decided at the last minute to audition for the group. Val had a singing voice that was about as melodic as a hyena's laugh. I tried to warn her, but Valarie's self-esteem was so high that unless it was some type of compliment or praise, anything I said to her usually went in one ear and flew out of the other.

She tried to pretend like it was no big deal when Ebony told her to 'sit her ass down' in the middle of her off-key performance, but I knew that she was burning up inside. Val hated getting dissed and she didn't take well to rejection.

While I was floating higher than a hot air balloon during the bus ride home, Val tried to pull me down with subtle slights about the group and our unlikelihood of success. It didn't matter, though. I was so excited that nothing, not even Val and her pettiness, was able to steal my joy.

I had been practicing with the group for about four months when a whirlwind blew into our rehearsal and introduced himself as Uncle Mervin.

We were practicing in Patrice's grandmother's living room when Mervin Jackson, Ms. Emma's oldest son, graced us with his presence. He was a tall, cocoa colored man, sporting a Jheri Curl that was held back with an orange rubber band. His Lee jeans were so tight that I could see the imprint of the coins in his front pocket. A fleur de lis tattoo peeked out of the rip on the sleeve of his dirty white tee shirt.

He spoke loud and so fast that I had to listen close to make sure he was speaking English. When he realized that we were forming a singing group his face lit up like the fourth of July.

"Music, ah yeah, that's my thang," he boasted. "But what y'all girls know 'bout music?" Y'all don't know 'bout no music...talkin' 'bout bein' a singin' group. Martha Reeves and the Vandellas, Diana Ross and the Supremes, The Shirelles, now those were some groups. They had the moves *and* the sounds. Y'all as good as them?"

"Uncle Mervin, those groups are as old as Methuselah," Essence joked.

"And we're even better than them, Uncle Mervin!" Patrice bragged. "Check this out!"

She counted down and we began harmonizing to a tune that we had been practicing for about a week called, *Whatever You Want*.

"Not bad. Not bad at all," Uncle Mervin said, bobbing his head. Jheri Curl juice flew every which a-way. "I might be able to do something with y'all."

Uncle Mervin knew a man, who knew a man, and was able to book a gig for us at Tipitina's—a little hole in the wall nightclub that was a must stop for any artist wishing to make a name for themselves in New Orleans.

We would be the opening act for Louisiana Purchase, a legendary local group that tore up the scene back in the day with their hit, 'Baby's Love.' We weren't getting paid and had been instructed to sing cover hits, as opposed to our original songs, but hey, it was a gig and we planned on making the most of the opportunity.

Verse eight: baby I'm a star

Uncle Mervin became our new manager and a fixture at our rehearsals. We never signed any official paperwork with him nor had a verbal agreement to declare him our manager, but somehow the title became his.

He just started showing up at our rehearsals and started giving us advice and fussing at us when we weren't doing things the way he thought we should. Once he was able to secure the Tipitina's gig for us, that just seemed to seal the deal, and he became the unofficial manager of L9.

We worked harder than we ever had. Our vocals became stronger, our moves tighter, and Uncle Mervin's girlfriend, Ronisha, put together matching red sequenced outfits that had us feeling sexy and ready to compete with groups the caliber of EnVogue.

Well, we might have thought that we were ready to take on the best, but according to Uncle Mervin, we weren't about to catch anybody's attention, no matter how good we sounded, if we just stood in the middle of the stage looking as stiff as ironing boards.

"Move your asses, move your asses," he kept repeating, as we sang snippets of our songs for him.

I'd never been the world's best dancer, but my dancing had gotten a tad bit better after countless hours of practice in front of the bathroom mirror. I mean, I wasn't trying out to be a Soul Train dancer anytime soon, but I was able to keep up with what the twins threw my way.

Patrice, on the other hand, Lord, that girl was a mess. She couldn't dance to save her soul. So, after about three hours of trying to teach her basic choreography we gave up and decided to just sway our hips and go heavy with the hand movements.

The night of the show was a haze of chaos. It didn't help matters that mama appeared overly suspicious and seemed to be watching me like a hawk.

Lynette, Val, and I had to come up with some convoluted story about meeting a group of kids from school for a study session just to get out of the house. I just prayed that mama wouldn't try calling the made-up phone number that I'd given her, checking up on us.

It took longer getting dressed than we expected, and we were almost late for our own gig.

Essence and Ebony looked softer and sexier, with their newly plucked eyebrows and MAC made up faces. Patrice looked as cute as always. I didn't know what the mirror had to say about me, but if I looked anything like I felt, a zombie from Michael Jackson's Thriller video could've been my doppelganger.

The nightclub wasn't much bigger than the living room at my house, but as we squeezed into the tiny dressing room and put the finishing touches on our makeup, it seemed as if there was a packed and anxious house out there waiting for us. Or rather, waiting for Louisiana Purchase, but hey, they were getting us whether they liked it or not.

And they *did* like it. When the lights went down and the spotlight illuminated on the four of us, a hush came over the crowd. Someone sitting at the bar yelled, "All right, na. Do the damn thing!"

The music started...da dum, dum, dum, and I belted out, *"Many say, that I'm too young..."* Then the girls joined in, *"...to let you know just where I'm coming from."*

We sang Aretha Franklin's, *Giving Him Something He Can Feel,* almost better than the queen herself. The crowd went wild. We followed it up with The Emotion's, *Don't Ask my Neighbor,* and then got the crowd moving with Labelle's, *Lady Marmalade.*

For the last song of our set, Patrice gave Uncle Mervin a wink, just like we practiced, and he slipped the sound technician a twenty-dollar bill to change our music. Instead of EnVogue's, *Hold On,* as we'd run through during the dress rehearsal, the intro to our song, *Whatever You Want,* flooded the club.

The audience was quiet when they first heard the melody. They were trying to figure out if they knew the song, but by the time the intro was deep into its groove, and we came in with the lyrics, they were swaying right along with us.

We left the stage amid loud applause and ovations, and by the time we made it back to the dressing room, I was shaking like a leaf on a tree. I even cried. I couldn't believe that my dream seemed to be coming true.

Uncle Mervin was an excited mess. He was talking so fast, and his Ninth Ward accent was so thick, that I was getting a headache trying to figure out the words that were coming out of his mouth. I stopped trying and quickly changed into my street clothes, and went out into the club to look for Val and Lynette.

As I slid through the crowd to where my girls were jumping up and down trying to get my attention, I could have sworn I saw my father in the crowd. But by the time I wiped the tears of joy out of my eyes and turned to get a closer, I realized that as usual, I was searching for someone who just wasn't there.

Verse nine: heaven help me

"**S**ister Tracey, did you hear me? I said, the next song that we are going over is, *Order My Steps*. What are you over here daydreaming about?"

Raymond Solomon, New Hope's choir director and resident diva, stood in front of me snapping his manicured fingers in my face. His high-pitched voice snapped me back to the here and now.

I wasn't sure how long he had been standing there, trying to coax me back into the moment, but it must have been a while considering the way he rolled his eyes and sashayed away from me.

"I'm so tired of people wasting my precious time," he mumbled.

I cut my eyes to the right. Just as I suspected, Lynette was over there trying her best to hold in a laugh. She and I were forever making fun of Raymond behind his back. His clothes were a constant target of ours. Today's outfit was blue and green checkered pants with a lime green Polo shirt. Coupled with his mannerisms, he was so over the top, it was hard not to laugh at him.

"I'm sorry, Ray," I said, trying to wipe the smile off my face.

"Don't be sorry, be a professional," he huffed, and walked toward the front of the choir stand.

I decided to take rehearsal a little more seriously. Ray was right. Nobody had time to waste; not when I could have been doing something more important with my time, like practicing with my group for our next gig. A gig that we were confident would come after the way we tore up the stage at Tipitinas.

It had been a week since our debut performance and I was having a hard time coming back from cloud nine. Ray, however, was unimpressed with my foray into the secular world. All he cared about was making sure that we didn't sound like a bunch of fools on Sunday morning and getting through rehearsal so that he could make it home in time to watch reality television.

"Don't be so hard on her, Ray," Greg piped in, coming to my rescue even though I never asked him to.

I shot him a side-eye glare. Every time I turned around Gregory Adams was there, smiling at me or trying to talk to me. He even joined the choir, even though he couldn't sing a lick, and I knew it was because he was trying to get closer to me.

He was a decent guy and even kind of cute, in a nerdy sort of way. He probably would be a good boyfriend for somebody. He just wasn't for me.

We went through the song until Ray declared we sounded as good as we were going to get. He grabbed his man bag and made his way down the center aisle.

As Raymond walked out, a specimen so fine walked through the door that I almost dropped my hymnal. Apparently, Ray felt the same way that I did, because he nearly caught a case of whiplash while turning to look back at the guy.

Half the girls in the choir were about to bum rush him to find out who he was, but Sister Baptiste saved us the trouble.

"Oh, JP, you finally made it," she gushed. "Everybody, I would like you to meet my son, Jean-Paul Baptiste."

I felt like I had died and gone to heaven. He was gorgeous. He had a head full of sandy colored curls, his skin was the color of caramel popcorn and his light brown eyes almost had me in a trance.

I heard him speaking—I think that he was saying that it was nice meeting us—but I was so enamored that I had to literally shake my head to clear my mind of all the floaty little hearts and unicorns that danced in front of my eyes.

I didn't know how, and I didn't know when, but I knew that somehow, I was going to make him mine.

Verse ten: got to get you into my life

*S*unday morning, I was out of bed before my alarm went off. Usually, it took at least thirty minutes of Ma-Me's hollering to finally get me moving, but I was so excited about the possibility of seeing JP that I was sitting on the couch, fully dressed in my Sunday best before Ma-Me came in to put the coffee on.

Even Val, who always came up with excuses whenever I invited her to Sunday morning services, wanted in on the action. She claimed that I had talked JP up so much that she just *had* to get a look at the guy who had me going gaga, but I kept my eye on Val because she usually had motives for everything she did.

By the time Lynette and I had positioned ourselves in the choir stand, I could tell that every female member of New Hope Baptist Church, between the ages of fourteen to twenty-one, had the exact same idea. Apparently, word about Sister Baptiste's gorgeous son got around because there were girls sitting in the pews that I hadn't seen since Jesus was a baby.

Reverend Howard was deep into his sermon, but if someone were to offer me a million dollars to repeat one word that he said, I would've been as broke as I was when I first step foot through the door. I couldn't concentrate on anything but JP. He sat at the end of the third row with a far-off gaze. I was curious to know what he was thinking about.

I must have been deep into my own thoughts because at first, I didn't feel Lynette jabbing me in the side with her bony elbow.

"Ouch...what is it?" I hissed at her.

Using her china as a pointer, she gestured in the direction of Valarie, who was sitting between mama and Ma-Me.

Val was clearing her throat continuously, trying to get my attention. When I finally looked her way, she nudged her head in the direction of JP and gave me the thumbs up sign.

"I know, right?" I mouthed to her and we both broke out in girlish laughter.

We barely got the sound out of our mouths before Ma-Me shot us a look that popped our giggles in the air like bubbles. We zipped our lips and attempted to focus on the word.

As soon as pastor gave the benediction, I rushed to the back to hang up my choir robe and hopefully get a word in with JP before he left. I figured that he would be riding home with his mother, so I would probably have a few minutes to formulate and then execute a plan.

"Hey, Tracey, wait up a minute," Greg yelled from behind me, stopping me in my tracks. I closed my eyes and took a deep breath.

Greg had been trying to get my attention all morning, but I ignored him. Didn't he know that there were vultures in the air, circling around *my* JP?

I opened my eyes and looked at him, "Yes, Greg? What is it?"

"I...I...I was just wondering if you wanted to catch a movie or something after church."

I took another deep breath. Greg was a nice enough guy. I just wasn't interested in him in that way. Why couldn't he see that? I didn't want to hurt his feelings, but he wasn't giving me much choice.

"Greg," I said, trying to talk and figure out what I was going to say at the same time, "I like you, I do, and I think that you and I can be really good friends. But that's about it. I'm sorry..." I trailed off.

"Yeah, that's okay. No big deal."

Greg hurried away from me. I felt bad and a part of me wanted to run behind him and do a better job of letting him down, but then I thought about JP and how I probably didn't have much time left.

Instead of running behind Greg, I turned in the opposite direction and ran towards JP.

I made my way to the front parking lot and spotted Sister Baptiste sliding behind her steering wheel. JP was standing on the side of the car, looking delicious, and talking to Val.

As soon as we got situated in the back of mama's Honda Accord, I whispered in Valarie's ear.

"What was that all about?"

"What was what about?" she asked innocently, but it was apparent that she knew what I was talking about.

"What were you talking to JP about?"

"Oh, that, I was just welcoming him to our church family."

"*Our* church family?" I asked incredulously. "You're not even a member of this church!"

"We're all brothers and sisters in Christ, Tracey," Val said and turned to look out of the window.

As we approached our neighboring houses, I couldn't help recalling the first time I met Valarie Boudreaux.

My family moved to New Orleans East when I was six years old; next door to the Boudreaux family. After years of working penny ante jobs on construction sites around the city, daddy secured a big-time construction job working on the roof of the Superdome. The significant spike in pay enabled my parents to pack up their meager belongings from their shabby house around the corner from Ma-Me's Ninth Ward eyesore. They purchased a four-bedroom house in the more upscale area of New Orleans East.

I remember the afternoon of the move as if it were yesterday. Mama and daddy were unloading the U-Haul truck and I was trying my best to stay out of the way when I heard a soft voice coming from the side of the truck.

"You like banana pudding?"

I looked around the truck, trying to find the source of such an unusual question, and I spotted a girl about my age, staring back at me. She had two ponytails that reached the middle of her back. She wore a peach colored dress that tied around her neck and sandals with flowers on them in the same shade of peach.

"What?" I asked.

I saw her looking at me, but her question was so confusing that it left me wondering if she was real or if she was some fantasy playmate that I had conjured up.

"Pudding?" she repeated, proving that she was real. "Do you like banana pudding? I have some if you want some."

I grinned broadly and nodded.

"Then come on," she motioned and we walked over to her house without saying another word.

I remembered that day like it was yesterday. Especially, the look on Mrs. Boudreaux's face when she realized that we had eaten the pudding that she made to take to her church's potluck dinner. She didn't whoop us, though, as I'm sure that Ma-Me, or even mama would have done. She simply asked Val why she ate the pudding when she was instructed not to. In response, Val shrugged her shoulders and told her mother that she took it because she wanted it.

That's the way Val is. She is a good person and a great friend, but Val takes what she wants. I just prayed that she didn't want JP.

Verse eleven: baby be mine

I spent the rest of the week trying to find out everything that I could about Jean-Paul Baptiste. I knew that he preferred being called JP and that he had the most handsome face that I had ever seen, but through countless phone calls and not so subtle inquiries, I also learned that he was nineteen years old (an older man) and that he was taking a semester off from college in an attempt to jumpstart his rap career.

Maybe that is a link that I can use, I figured. We both had plans to make a name for ourselves in the music industry. I just needed to figure out a way to talk to him so that he could see how much we have in common.

Patrice picked me up after school in Uncle Mervin's baby blue Chevy, his pride and joy, and I wasn't even fully buckled in before I started picking her brain, hoping she could give me some advice on how to get JP to notice me.

"Whoa," she teased, "this boy must be some kind of fine. I've never seen you this way before."

"Yeah, he is the bomb," I admitted. "The problem is everybody else thinks so as well. I need to figure out a way to get him to see me."

"Alright, Tracey," she said, "let's get you to the house. When we get through with you, he'll be running behind you and not the other way around."

Patrice deftly maneuvered around the potholes in front of her grandmother's house and parked the Chevy in its designated spot under the carport. We made our way through the side door to the room off the kitchen, where we usually held our rehearsals.

"Hey dere, na! Y'all 'bout to make some pretty music?" Ms. Emma, Patrice's grandmother, smiled her toothless grin at us as we walked into the room. She was standing at the sink, cleaning turnip greens and listening to a taped sermon. I walked over and gave her a kiss on her wrinkled cheek.

Five minutes later, Ebony and Essence came in. Patrice filled them in on my dilemma and we all got down to the business at hand. Operation Snag JP had begun.

By the time I made it to choir rehearsal, I looked like a totally different chick. Patrice took my hair out of the boring ponytail that I had worn to school. She curled and styled it until it was bouncing and behaving just like the women on TV. Ebony gave me a manicure and Essence spruced up my attire by trading out my uniform blouse for one of Patrice's fitted tee shirts. Their last-minute advice to me was to sit back, chill out, and wait for him to come to me.

When I stepped through the doors of the sanctuary, I could feel almost every eye on me. Well, almost every eye. As soon as I sat down next to him Greg started acting as if last week's church program was the most interesting thing in the world. His head was bowed, as if he was studying every word in it, and he refused to make eye contact with me. I felt bad. I knew that he was hurt by the way that I'd handled his movie invitation last week, but then I had to remind myself that I'd done nothing wrong. It wasn't my fault if I didn't like him in the same way that he liked me.

We were halfway through rehearsal when JP came sauntering in. He folded his long body into the same pew that he sat on during Sunday service and watched us practice. I wasn't sure if he was simply waiting for his mother or if he saw something, or someone, in the choir stand that caught his eye. Regardless of the reason, he appeared less bored than he had during Sunday service.

After rehearsal, I was forced to make small talk with Dawanna and LaShon, since Lynette was home in bed with a stomach bug and hadn't come to practice. Though I was about the same age as the girls we didn't have much in common, so there wasn't much for us to talk about.

I could tell that they were both crushing on JP by the way they were sneaking glances and giggling at him. LaShon even had the nerve to ask me if I had gotten all dolled up to try to catch JP's attention. I gave her the stink-eye and didn't answer her question.

Instead, I excused myself and went to the restroom to check my hair and lip gloss.

By the time I made it back from the restroom I noticed that almost everyone had already left. I hadn't realized how long I had been gone, primping and dreaming. I walked to the front of the building and looked for mama, who was supposed to be picking me up, but she was nowhere in sight. I wondered if she'd forgotten me.

I was about to go back inside and give her a call, but Greg stopped me.

"Hi, Tracey," he said, acting all shy and as if he hadn't been sitting next to me and ignoring me all night.

"Hi, Greg," I returned. I took one look at his sad eyes and I wanted a chance to explain to him why I said no when he asked me out. "Hey, is it okay if I talked to you for a minute?"

"Yeah, sure," he said. We moved over to a quiet corner of the vestibule.

"About last Sunday," I started, but Greg shook his head.

"Don't worry about it," he said. "You don't owe me any explanations." And then he changed the subject. "What are you still doing here, anyway? Are you waiting for a ride?"

"Yes," I admitted. "With Lynette being home sick, I guess my mom forgot to come and pick me up."

"If you need a ride, I'll be happy to—"

"Tracey, right?" said a voice from behind.

It was JP. I hadn't seen him standing there. His smile was wide. His eyes mesmerizing. His presence overwhelming.

I have no way of knowing for sure, but I'm sure I looked goofy as I nodded robotically.

"I'll be glad to take you home if you need a ride," JP offered.

"Okay," I uttered and followed JP to his mother's car like he was the pied piper. I left Greg standing there dumbfounded with his keys dangling in his hands.

Verse twelve: all I could do is cry

"So, how did you know my name?" I finally asked. My voice was shakier and higher pitched than ever.

"You'd be surprised at what I know," JP answered with a bad boy smirk.

His sandy colored, curly hair made him look like a little boy, but the way he looked at me made me know that he did not have little boy thoughts.

I could feel my insides turning to liquid.

"I know what you don't know," I sassed, trying to pretend that being alone with him was no big deal. "You don't know where I live because you just passed up my exit."

He laughed and then said, "Well, I was hoping that we could spend some time together. Get to know one another better before I drop you off. Is that okay, or is your mother expecting you at home?"

"She must not be too concerned about me since she forgot to pick me up," I answered. "So, I guess it's okay if we hang out for a little while."

"Cool," he said and reached over to turn the radio up. Some rap song that I had never heard before played while. I sat in Sister Baptiste's Cadillac smiling like a loon. I couldn't believe that I was spending one-on-one time with JP. I felt like my prayers had been answered.

JP steered the car into the entrance to City Park. I could feel myself getting nervous all over again. He was older, and probably a lot more experienced, than I was. I hoped I would be able to hold my own with him.

He parked in an isolated spot next to a massive moss-covered tree and turned the music down. A group of guys were shooting baskets and trash-talking a few feet away from us, but other than that, it seemed as if JP and I had the whole park to ourselves.

He lowered the window a little. Within minutes, the humidity wrapped around me like a blanket. It was only April, but the temperature was already in the eighties and I could feel the *kitchen* in the back of my head starting to curl up. I nervously patted it down, hoping that Patrice's cute hairstyle would hold.

"So, Ms. Tracey," he said as he folded a piece of gum into his mouth, "word on street is that you are quite the little songstress."

"Word on the street," I joked.

"Okay, word in the church," he laughed.

I laughed along with him.

"I'm not sure if you heard," he said, "but you are looking at New Orleans' next rap superstar right here.

Once my album drops, I'ma be bigger than C-Murder and Master P put together. Shoot, I'm 'bout to give all No Limit *and* Cash Money a run for their money!"

I wasn't sure how to respond to his enthusiasm, but it didn't matter because JP went on talking about himself as if he didn't need or expect me to participate in the conversation.

"My moms thinks that I'm going back to school next semester," he continued, "but by then I'll probably be touring with my dudes. Tearin' this mutha up! Whatchu think about that?"

Again, he didn't give me a chance to answer. Instead, he unfastened his seatbelt and scooted a little closer to me.

"Why are you sitting all the way over there? Come a little closer so I can get to know you better."

I inched my body closer to his and in one fluid motion JP had his arms around me.

"I knew from the first time I saw you that you weren't like the rest of those lil' church girls," he said. "I knew you were somebody who knew how to let loose and have a good time."

I wasn't sure what to make of JP's comment. I knew he thought that was a compliment, but to my ears it felt like an underhanded insult. Was he trying to say that he thought I was easy?

I pulled away slightly, trying to figure out how to get everything back on track, but then JP started kissing me. A deep, sexy kiss that seemed to set off every one of my nerve endings. He tasted like Juicy Fruit and felt like paradise and bliss all rolled into one.

"Girl, this is what I've been waiting for since the moment I laid eyes on you. I knew that you would feel like this," he mumbled into my neck.

Again, the cat held my tongue.

"Let's hop in the back," JP suggested. "That way we can get a little more comfortable."

I wasn't sure that was such a great idea. I liked JP, a lot, but I really didn't know him. Most of all, I didn't know what he expected of me.

"What about your mother?" I asked, trying to find a way to slow things down. "Isn't she expecting you to come back with her car?

"My moms is in a meeting with some of those church folks, and you know how they like to talk. We got lots of time."

JP was moving and talking at the same time. He hopped out of the car and made himself comfortable in the backseat. I reluctantly got out and joined him.

"Yeah, this is much better," he said and folded me into his arms. And then before I knew it, he was laying full length on top of me, grinding into my pelvis. I could feel his *thing* getting hard underneath the thin cotton of his basketball shorts.

I felt myself losing control of the situation and I desperately wanted to get up and tell him that this was all moving too fast, but I couldn't. It just felt too good. Instead, I began rolling underneath him, trying to catch up to his rhythm.

Then he lifted my tee shirt up, exposing my bra. It snapped from the front, and JP deftly unhooked it, sending my breasts spilling all over the place.

He wrapped his hand around one of them and began squeezing and tugging on it. He then took it into his mouth and began sucking and slurping on it, while trying to remove his shorts at the same time. This was moving way too fast!

46

I tried saying no, that I needed more time to think about this, but when I opened my mouth to speak JP smoothly slipped his tongue inside and all I was able to get out was an inaudible moan.

"JP, wait a minute," I was finally able to get out. "I don't want this. Not like this."

"Girl, you know you want it," he moaned.

"I could tell by the way you were looking at me. Stop tryna pretend that this ain't what you had in mind the minute you stepped foot in my car. It's okay, though, lil' songbird. We ain't gotta tell nobody 'bout this. This here gonna stay between you and me," he said as he pushed my panties to the side and thrust himself inside of me.

verse thirteen: ball confusion

I didn't let JP take me home. Instead, I rearranged my clothing and stepped out of his mother's car in slow motion, as if I was moving through molasses. He half-heartedly asked if I still needed a ride home, but I didn't answer him. Instead, I kept walking.

I staggered to the bus stop in a haze of disbelief. My mind was so messed up that I couldn't decide what to focus on first: the realization that my virginity had just been snatched from me or the fact that I could have been so naïve and stupid for believing that JP was one of the good guys. Hell, I felt stupid for believing that good guys even existed at all.

Surprisingly, I did not cry. I guess I was too numb for tears. Instead, I leaned my sore and weary body against the bus stop pole and wrapped my arms tightly across my chest.

Thank goodness I didn't have to wait long before the bus pulled up to my stop. I boarded behind a haggard looking middle-aged lady who appeared as if she was on her way to her one hundredth job and plopped down on a seat near the front of the bus.

As a result of mama and Ma-Me's over protectiveness, I could count on one hand the number of times that I had ridden on public transportation. I took a furtive glance around, taking in the overweight Caucasian bus driver, the working mom, and three teenage boys hanging out at the back of the bus, and sent up a quick prayer of thanks that at least the bus was almost empty and relatively quiet.

I leaned my head against the window and closed my eyes, attempting to block out the sound of JP's voice and the look on his face when he shoved himself inside of me.

"Umm, excuse me young lady," said the bus driver, "this is the end of the line. Did you miss your stop?"

I woke up to the sound of the bus driver speaking to me, but I was too disoriented to make any sense out of his words. I sat up straight and winced at the crook that was forming in my neck from falling asleep against the window. I hesitantly turned my body and confirmed what I already suspected; I was the last passenger on the bus and I had no idea where I was.

"Where am I?" I asked, trying to disguise the panic that was quickly building up in me.

"This is North Miro Street. Lower Ninth Ward."

I made no move to exit the bus, so he repeated what he'd said earlier.

"End of the line."

I stared at him, staring at me. I knew that he was waiting for me to get up and get off so that he could finish his shift, but I was scared, broke, and had no idea how I was going to get home.

After a few more minutes passed the bus driver loudly cleared his throat and I knew there was no more postponing the inevitable. I got up and began making my way off the bus.

It had been years since I'd been in this part of town. The Ninth Ward had a reputation of being a dangerous, crime ridden area even back in the days when Lynette and I were little kids playing on those streets, but nowadays you couldn't turn on the news or open a newspaper without hearing about some murderous vendetta or drug deal gone wrong in the area. I knew that I needed to get back to my own neck of the woods quick, fast, and in a hurry.

"Think, Tracey, think," I mumbled, trying to formulate a quick plan of action.

I had to find a phone so that I could call someone to pick me up, but I didn't have any money and there was no way that I was going to go up and ask some random stranger on the street to lend me a quarter.

My feet started moving before my brain had a chance to catch up, and before I knew it, I was standing on a block that seemed familiar to me—Ma-Me's.

The house looked exactly as I'd remembered it; like a narrow gray eyesore resting proudly in the sky as if it was the most majestic structure in the world. With one glance, my mind tried to revisit the unhappy memories that I had of the place.

I recalled the days following mama and daddy's divorce and the uncertainty and sadness that was all-consuming to me at the time. I shook those negative thoughts away and willed myself to counter them with recollections of the fun and good times that I had growing up inside that house.

I remembered climbing the huge fig tree in the backyard to get to the biggest, juiciest fruit. I remembered falling from said tree and the look of unadulterated panic on Ma-Me's face as she raced to make sure that I was alright.

It was pure love that I saw on her face. And even though I was still convinced that she favored Lynette over me, in that moment I knew that her love for me was real and unfaltering. Suddenly, there was not a thing in the world that I wanted more than to get home to the familiarity of Ma-Me's scowl.

Closing my eyes tight and taking a deep breath, I tried to clear my mind and get my wits about me. Where could I go? What could I do? I looked up one end of the street and saw five teenaged boys in a tight circle, some standing and some squatting, probably shooting dice. I turned and looked down the other end of the street and I saw some girls jumping Double Dutch. I started walking towards the girls.

After a few steps, I hesitated and then stopped in my tracks. It sounded as if somebody was trying to get my attention. I paused for a couple of seconds and then I heard it again. I turned and saw a disheveled looking man stepping out of the shadows of an alleyway. His torn t-shirt was so dirty and gray that it was hard to guess what color it had been when it was taken fresh out the package, and his filthy jeans were at least four inches too long and frayed at the hem.

"Say girl, you have a dollar, or two...or twenty?" he asked, chucking at his own wittiness.

Answer? Don't answer? Walk away calmly? Run like the wind? A million questions raced through my mind and the answers weren't coming to me fast enough.

I decided that calm was the best way to proceed. I continued walking, pretending that I hadn't heard him talking to me.

Big mistake. He started walking behind me.

"Say girl, I know you heard me. What, you think you too good to talk to the likes of me?"

"No," I said, but I wasn't even sure which one of his questions I was answering. I kept walking, this time a little faster.

"No, you don't have the money, or no, you don't think you too good?"

I didn't answer, just kept moving to my unknown destination.

"'Cause you prob'ly is too good," he continued. "That's okay, though. I could be good to you too," he said, smiling his snaggle-toothed grin at me.

He started walking a little faster. "That's what you want? You want me to be good to you?"

I started running. He ran behind me. I opened my mouth and let out a scream that I wasn't sure that I would be able to stop.

Verse fourteen: a child with the blues

Ma-Me tiptoed into my bedroom and placed the back of her hand against my forehead. I guess she called herself trying not to disturb me, but she was talking so loud that even if I had been asleep there was no way that I would have stayed that way.

"Well, she ain't carryin' a fever. I guess that's good, but something is shole nuff wrong with dis girl. The way she's been mopin' and draggin' all over da place for days now. Diane, you might need to take her to dat hospital of yours for a check-up."

My eyes flew open! The last thing I needed was for mama to take me to the doctor.

"Ma-Me, what are you doing in here?" I asked, all groggy sounding. Pretending that I was just waking up out of a sound sleep.

She and mama were standing on the side of my bed, obviously worried about me. Mama was still in her hospital scrubs and her hair was pulled back in a ponytail. She looked young, more like my big sister than my mother.

"I'm just checkin' on ya," Ma-Me said. "Makin' sure that you ain't sick."

I was about to tell them that I was fine, just tired or something like that, but then I remembered that it was Sunday. If I said that I was fine they would expect me to get up and get ready for church. There was no way that I could step foot in that church and face JP.

"I'm not feeling great. Must be a bug that's going around or something."

"Anh hunh, I knew it," Ma-Me said, shuffling out of the door.

I figured she going to make some goose grease and honey or some other concoction that she was always trying to pour down our throats whenever Lynette or I got sick. I shuddered just thinking about it.

Mama sat on the edge of my bed. She felt my forehead the same as Ma-Me had done.

"Tracey, baby, are you sure you don't need to see a doctor? Ma-Me is right, you don't have a fever, but your eyes look glassy to me."

Probably because I had been up crying all night.

"No, mama," I reassured her. "Go on and get ready for church. I'm sure I'll feel better soon."

As soon as they left for church, I sat up on the side of my bed. I didn't need Ma-Me's nasty medicine. What I needed was my innocence back, and there was nothing that anyone could do to make that happen.

The phone rang, but I just looked at it. Didn't even think about answering. I knew that it was Greg. I owed him an explanation. That much was for sure.

After I ran away from that perverted homeless man in the Ninth Ward, I ran to the group of girls who were jumping Double Dutch and begged one of them to let me use her phone. Without even thinking about it, I called Greg. So yeah, he deserved to know why I called him in the middle of the night to pick me up from the Ninth Ward, of all places. He deserved to know why I looked so disheveled and distraught, and why I sat in his car and cried the whole way home.

He deserved to know, but not now. Now, I just needed to forget.

Verse fifteen: damaged

eeks later, my mind was still messed up. To make matters worse, I had a feeling that I was pregnant after waking up two days in a row feeling like Hurricane Camille was going on inside of my stomach. And when Ma-Me plopped down at the breakfast table and announced that she had a dream about frying fish, I excused myself from the table, threw on the same clothes that I had worn the day before and went to Walgreens to buy a pregnancy test.

I walked down the aisles of the drugstore as if I was still at home in my bed, in the middle of a bad dream.

What am I going to do? I kept thinking.

Mama was sure to have a heart attack and attack me if she found out I was pregnant. I didn't even want to think about how Ma-Me would react, not to mention everybody at church. I grabbed the test, threw three crumpled five-dollar bills at the clerk and raced home to find out my future.

After sneaking into the house with the bag tucked under my shirt, I ran to the bathroom and ripped open the package. I sat on the toilet with my head dangling between my legs and kept repeating to myself, "Negative is good. Negative is good."

I kept my eyes riveted to that plastic stick, barely blinking, and almost jumped for joy when I saw the pink negative sign in the display window. But before I could even start my celebration, the minus sign morphed into a plus, and I knew that life, as I knew it, was over.

I sat there for about twenty minutes, trying to figure out what to do. For the first time in my life, I felt totally alone. I thought about talking to Lynette but though we were only thirteen months apart in age, I prided myself on trying to be a good big sister and a role model to her. How was I going to look going to my little sister, and not only admitting to her that I was pregnant, but also that I was probably the biggest fool in New Orleans.

I thought about Ma-Me's no nonsense talk with me about sex. I guess she felt that mama wasn't doing a good enough job, talking about chastity and commitment and stuff like that, so Ma-Me came bursting through my bedroom door one afternoon and dropped down onto my bed.

"Look girl," she said, "this whole sex thing is easy enough to figure out. Bottom line is, the hole plus the pole, equals a baby. You got dat?"

Mama and I sat there staring at Ma-Me. I knew that Ma-Me didn't believe in beating around the bush, but I had never heard her that raw.

Mama finally found her voice and scolded Ma-Me for butting into our conversation and talking so frankly to me, but Ma-Me just kept on looking at me as if she expected an answer to her question.

"You got it?"

Finally, I said, "Yes, Ma-Me. I got it."

Apparently, I hadn't gotten it. Because despite everything I knew to be true, I still found myself facing the likelihood of being a teenaged mother.

Verse sixteen: backstabbers

I knew the only person I could turn to was JP. At first, I was nervous about telling him, but by the time I made it across town to his house, I had convinced myself that although he wouldn't be happy with the news, the least he would do is help me figure out a way out of this mess.

I pulled up in front of Sister Baptiste's house and parked my mama's car at the curb next to her silver Cadillac. A shiver ran through me. I couldn't help but remember what happened the last time I was in that car.

I ran a hand through my tangled hair, applied and blotted Wet n' Wild lip gloss, and set off to do what I'd gone there for.

I stepped out of the car and started walking up the walkway, but stopped when I saw something that completely blew my mind. Valarie was stepping out of JP's house with a smile on her face so big you'd think she'd won the lottery.

JP walked out behind her and gave her a quick swat on her behind before they even realized I was there. I blinked my eyes twice, sure that I must have been seeing things, but when I refocused, Val was walking right past me as if I was invisible. She hopped into her mother's car and slowly buckled her seat belt. She even stared at me and gave me a little smirk before speeding off.

"Tracey, what you doin' here?" JP asked.

I ignored him and got back in the car.

I must have gotten back home on cruise control, because I don't remember starting the ignition or steering the wheel. Before I knew it, I was parked in my driveway, looking at my house as if I had never seen it before. I wondered if I would even be welcomed in there ever again after they found out about my condition.

I was amazed at how fast my life could change. Not even a month ago, I was practicing with L9 and dreaming about a life of fortune and fame. Now, after one mistake, it looked like the only thing in my future was diapers and formula.

I made my way to my room, smoothed out my red and black stripped bed spread, and sat down. I had never felt so tired in my entire life. Then I thought about something that mama said to me, a long time ago.

"Don't ever think that you can do something that I won't find out about, sooner or later."

I shuttered at the thought, but I knew that it was true.

I waited until mama left for her 3 to 11 shift and then I put the pregnancy test and a note that read: *I'm sorry,* on her pillow.

I went to bed and waited for the shit to hit the fan.

Around midnight, I smelled her before I even heard her come into my room. She had been drinking, and I hadn't seen mama sipping on anything stronger than a Coke since daddy left. I was about to sit up and begin begging for her forgiveness, but before I could work up the courage, she slipped into my bed and put her arms around me.

"We'll get through this," she slurred, as her warm, salty tears fell on the back of my neck.

Part Two

Verse seventeen: baby's love

"Please, mama. I'ca have some cereal? Pleeezeee?"
She asked for about the millionth time and tugged on the hem of my skirt.

I placed my mascara wand on my cracked Formica countertop and took a deep breath.

Lord, this child is driving me crazy, I thought. *I had already cooked a very delightful meal of Hamburger Helper and creamed corn earlier this evening, which she'd hardly touched, and now she decides to wait until I'm ready to run out of the door to start begging me for food.*

"Jazz," I said slowly and calmly, trying my best not to take my frustration out on my daughter. After all, it wasn't her fault that I'd spent so much time on the phone fussing with Carson, that I only left myself twenty minutes to get dressed for work. "First of all, "I'ca" is not a word. You are supposed to say, 'May I please have some cereal.'"

"Ok. May I please have some cereal?" Jazz asked, smiling sweetly and showing the dimple in her left cheek. Looking just like me.

"I'm sorry, baby," I said, scooping her into my arms and almost throwing out my back in the process.

I shook my head with wonder at how big my child had gotten. I found it hard to believe that she had been in my life for over four years now. It seems like she was born only yesterday. And though it's been indescribably hard at times, I can barely remember a time when she wasn't here taking up all my time and all my heart.

"Mama is going to be late for work," I said. "I'm sure that Granny or Ma-Me will give you some cereal once you get to their house."

"Alright, Mommy. I'ca just eat at Ma-Me's house," she said and ran off to her room.

I named my baby girl, Jazzmine Elizabeth Dubois, but everybody simply called her Jazz.

I feel that one of the most loving and important things that a mother can do for her child is to give them a name that compliments them. The name that you give your child will follow them for their entire life. Hell, sometimes it does more than follow them, sometimes it even goes before them.

Imagine an employer picking up a resume and seeing some nonsense like Apple Johnson or Prince Michael Smith. You know doggone well that they are just going to shake their heads, let out a quick little chuckle, and throw that mess directly into file thirteen—the trash can.

My best friend Kenya and I kept a running list of crazy names. We started the list one day while we shopped in the mall and heard someone, just as loud and country as they wanted to be, yell out, "Tobynisha! Get over here girl!"

Kenya and I looked at one another and almost fell out laughing. Ever since then, whenever one of us came across a name that sounded weird or too outrageous to be true, we promptly called the other and added it to our list.

Silly, I know. But that's what true friends are. Someone that you can trust enough to be silly with. And Kenya was the epitome of a true friend. The extreme opposite of Valarie who had never been a friend to me at all.

As a matter of fact, Valarie did such a number on me that I almost missed out on one of my biggest blessings: Kenya.

Besides Lynette, Kenya was the only person that knew the truth about Jazzmine's conception. I'd sworn them both to secrecy. They were the only two people in the world whom I could talk honestly to and confide that I had no clue as to what I was doing, what the new vision for my life was, and how I planned on being someone's mama.

I was asked to leave the praise and worship team at church when my belly became too round to hide behind my lavender choir robe. Kenya embraced me as I was going through that difficult and embarrassing time in my life. She laughed with me, cried with me— which was often during those first few months—and was there with me, holding my hand when my little sweet pea, Jazzmine, was born.

Kenya studied at Louisiana State University and interned at a private school, YES Academy, as a teaching assistant. She loved every minute of it.

I'm not going to lie. I was a little bit jealous of her. Let me be clear, I wasn't jealous of her per se, I was happy that my girl was working towards her goals. I guess I envied the fact that she was building a career without the burdens of parenthood. I wished I could've done the same thing.

During our weekly telephone chats, I could practically reach out and touch Kenya's excitement as she described the classes that she took. I could hear the passion in her voice as she talked about the students in her class. It inspired me.

Her stories were also a source of amusement because working in education gave her lots of entries for our 'Crazy Name List'.

One day, she called me laughing so hard that she could hardly get her words out.

"Sit down, Tracey," she said. "I have a good one for you."

I instantly knew what she was talking about.

"Okay, let me have it," I said, starting to laugh before she even told me the name.

"Slick Rick," she blurted out.

"Huh?" I asked, still laughing, but mostly confused.

"Slick Rick," she repeated.

"Somebody's name is Slick Rick?" I asked incredulously, almost falling out of my chair.

"Yep. Slick Rick Antoine Montgomery."

"Nope. You're lying. I know doggone well that some trifling mama did not name her baby, Slick Rick."

"Well, you better believe it because I am looking at a copy of his birth certificate as we speak."

"Dang, that's messed up. That poor child doesn't stand a chance," I said before we hung up the phone so that Kenya could get back to work.

Slick Rick Montgomery. That is the reason that I took so much care in naming my own child. I wanted to give her a name that she could grow into, as well as a name that represented something important to me. Hence the name, Jazzmine Elizabeth. Jazzmine, to represent my love for music—all types of music, but especially the passion and unfaltering grove that can be felt when listening to a great jazz piece. And Elizabeth because it is my mama's middle name, and I wanted my daughter to know the importance of strong family ties and the unconditional love that her family will make sure she feels for the rest of her life.

My singing career with L9 slowly, but eventually, fizzled out once I progressed further along in my pregnancy. After our Tipitina's debut we were able to book a few paying gigs at parties and clubs around the city, but the rounder my belly got, the harder it got for me to squeeze into that little red sequenced outfit and try to look and sound sexy.

Mama insisted I go to college after I had the baby, to Southern University at New Orleans or even a community college like Delgado, and she and Ma-Me would make sure that Jazz was taken care of as I went about my studies. But instead, I opted to find a full-time job, move into an inexpensive two-bedroom apartment, and tried to make a life for me and my child.

I worked as a cashier at a grocery store for a little while, then I worked at The Bank of America as a bank teller, but about six months after I started at the bank, I lucked up and was offered a gig singing a few hours a week at Harrah's Casino. The pay sucked, but my manager kept dangling the carrot of a pay increase in front of my face.

That day had better come soon, I often thought as I threw pajamas and a purple and green stripped short set into Jazz's overnight bag. *Because at this point, a sister barely has a pot to piss in or a window to throw it out.*

Verse eighteen: on my own

I barely have words to describe how I feel about JP, other than he was a manipulative, sorry, pathetic excuse of a man. I guess those words are as good a start as any, but they don't even begin to scratch the surface of what I think about Jean-Paul Baptiste.

I know, it sounds like I am bitter, but I promise, I'm not. Yeah, he treated me like crap. Yeah, he used up my body, stomped on my heart, and then that cocky dog did not even act fazed when he found out I was pregnant. But in order to snatch a crumb of sanity for myself, I had to let it all go. I realize that I may not be able to control everything that happens to me, but I can control the way I react to it.

Ma-Me's words still ring in my ears from the time surrounding the days that I discovered I was pregnant and found out the truth about JP and Valarie.

I was moping around the house, crying about the way he took advantage of me and the way that Valarie betrayed me. Though Ma-Me didn't know all the gory details, she knew that I was hurt and that Val and I were no longer friends.

One day, she overheard me tell Lynette how mad I was that Val had gone behind my back and lied to me. Ma-Me made her way into the room, glared at me and said, "Look girl, a lie ain't shit to tell."

She walked back into her room, biting into a luncheon meat sandwich, as if she hadn't just uttered the words that would redefine every truth that I had ever known.

Her words were harsh, but she was right. It was a hard pill to swallow, but I quickly came to realize that there was nothing special about me or my situation. People are messed over and lied to everyday of the week. I'm not the first female that's been abused by a man, and unless the world stops spinning tomorrow, I'm sure that I won't be the last.

What ticked me off the most, though, is that JP had the nerve to act like nothing happened when he saw me. He strolled into church as if he didn't have a care in the world. As if he hadn't turned my life upside down.

And then, to make matters worse, when he finally saw Jazzmine for the first time, as I was strolling her through the mall, he had the nerve to take one quick glance inside her stroller, suck his top teeth with his bottom lip, and sneer at me.

69

"You bet not be going around telling people that she's mine," he said before turning to walk away.

He had me wondering how I was ever able to fix mind into thinking that he was cute.

He was arrogant enough to call about a year later talking about his music career didn't pan out the way he expected it to and that he'd found Jesus. He said he wanted a chance to get to know his daughter.

"Go kick rocks," is what I told him. "Being a sperm donor, an unwanted sperm donor at that, does not make you a father. Besides, there is no way in hell I'm going to let you in my daughter's life just so you can inflict as much pain on her as you did to me."

It's all good, though. Jazzmine's got all the love and adoration she needed from me, mama, Lynette, Kenya and even grouchier than ever, Ma-Me.

I'm not going lie, though. It cracked my heart a little every time Jazzmine asked me about her daddy. Why he wasn't around to sing Happy Birthday to her or bring her a doll at Christmas.

I know some trifling heifers like to make a sport out of dogging their baby-daddies to their children, but that wasn't me. Laying out a man's bad business and whorish ways doesn't make you look like a better woman. You must admit that you are just like the rest of us—you took a gamble with love and lost.

Regardless of how much I couldn't stand JP, to part my lips and tell my baby that her father took one look at her and walked off without a glance back, would only hurt her. And hurting my child was something I vowed I would never do.

Verse nineteen: Dr. Feelgood

Monday morning and I am racing around the apartment like the Tazmanian devil. Kenya called me last week and told me that her cousin knows someone whose office was in immediate need of help.

"Yes!" I yelled before she was able to finish the sentence.

She didn't have to ask me twice. My money was funny, my savings were nonexistent, and I was in desperate need of a full-time job.

I had an interview as a receptionist at Baker and Brewer, an advertising firm downtown in the heart of the CBD, and it was imperative that I make it there on time.

"Where in the heck is my other shoe?" I muttered, shuffling from my bedroom to Jazz's room, looking under beds and in closets for my other black pump.

To say I was exhausted was an understatement. After performing two sets at Harrah's before grabbing a late bite to eat with Carson the night before, my head barely hit the pillow before the alarm jarred me awake again.

On top of that, the apartment was a mess, as usual, and I made a mental note to at least attempt to straighten up as soon as I got back home. Between work, dating Carson, and trying to spend quality time with Jazzmine, I had little spare time. The rare occasions where I could find a moment for myself were so precious to me that cleaning the house was the last thing on my mind.

I stopped racing around for a second and let my mind drift back to Carson. My latest, not-so love interest.

I like him, most times, but something about him won't let me take that leap. Mama called me a crazy fool and said I had better *learn* to love him.

I can hear her now, whispering in my ear after I introduced her to Dr. Carson Carter.

"It's just as easy to love rich as it is to love poor," she said before shaking his hand and inviting him to sit down for a bowl of shrimp stew.

Carson is a good guy. Besides being a gifted oncologist at Ochsner hospital, he is extremely affectionate and considerate; often dropping over with thoughtful *just because* gifts like flowers for me and cute little teddy bears or dolls for Jazzmine.

And if that isn't enough, he was quite pleasant to look at. Six feet with walnut brown skin, a cropped haircut, and goatee.

We literally bumped into one another as I was taking Ma-Me to a doctor's appointment. Ma-Me, in her infinite wisdom, decided that riding in the elevator and walking down the lobby of the hospital was the perfect opportunity to lecture me, yet again, about not spending enough time with Jazzmine.

"Look, girl," she scolded, "I know dat you working hard and tryna do what's right by yo' chile. I'm just saying dat you gon haf'ta do a little betta, dat's all. A chile needs her mama."

"I know, Ma-Me," I said, trying to pacify her and gently knock her off her soap box, wondering for about the millionth time how I got stuck with the task of bringing Ma-Me to her doctor's appointment.

She continued as if I hadn't said a word. "Diane and I love dat chile to death, you know we do, but can't nobody take the place of mama. And believe it or not, Ma-Me is not always gon' be here. Shoot, just last night I was cleaning up in the living room and dat ole cuckoo clock dat that hadn't worked in about ten years just started clucking away. Nearly scared the life outta me."

I rolled my eyes to the ceiling and uttered a question that I was sure that I would regret asking.

"What does that mean? What does an old clock have to do with anything, Ma-Me?"

"What dat mean?" she asked incredulously, raising her voice and looking at me as if I had just asked the most ridiculous question that she'd ever heard.

"When a broked clock suddenly chimes dat means dat there is gonna be a death in the family. Dat's what dat mean!"

I took in a deep breath and let it out slowly. I was not about to go down that road with Ma-Me.

I was so annoyed and distracted that I completely overlooked the handsome doctor who had stopped in his tracks directly in front of me. Before I knew what was happening, I was colliding into his back, causing him to drop the file that he had been looking at.

"Oh my gosh, I am so sorry!" I said, bending down to help him pick up his scattered papers.

"Yeah...whatever," he snapped and then bent down to pick up his papers, completely dismissing me.

I was just about to decide whether I was about to apologize again, or go off on him for being so rude, when he looked up at me and his whole demeanor softened.

I decided to go with the second apology. "No, really, I apologize," I said. "I should have been looking where I was going."

"No worries." He said, this time with a smile. "But you know...you can make this all up to me by letting me take you to dinner tonight."

I was flattered. A good-looking doctor was asking me out to dinner. But I was also terrified. For the past four years, I had made Jazzmine my entire life. Sure, I'd been out on a few dates here or there, but after the ordeal with JP, I was afraid to trust myself and my instincts. Let alone trusting someone else.

My first date with Carson was not exactly what I thought it was going to be. I was so amped up about going out with a rich, sexy doctor that I guess I expected him to show up in a tuxedo with dozens of roses in the back of his limousine or something. I certainly didn't expect him to be wearing mom jeans and driving an unimpressive Toyota Corolla. Instead of a bouquet of roses he had three lilies, which he placed in my lap after I sat in the car.

He was also as boring as all get out. He spent most of the night talking about his patients and his mishaps on the golf course. When it was finally my turn to speak, I told him a little about Jazzmine and my stagnant singing career. After that our conversation resorted to nonsensical chit-chat, occasional unh hunhs, and then an uncomfortable silence.

Because I didn't have anything else going on, and because I knew that I would hear mama's mouth if I didn't, I went on a few more dates with him. They were better than the first, that's for sure. After giving him a second, and then a third chance, I realized that he was actually a very sweet guy. Sometimes he'd say something so lame and unexpected that it was quite funny. He was beginning to grow on me.

He was thirty-two years old, ten years older than I am, but at age of 32 he has accomplished so much more than most of the men I know will get done in their entire lives. He's from Virginia, but wound up in New Orleans via a medical residency at Charity Hospital. Maybe that is what's missing—that New Orleans flavor. I don't know, but I do know that *something* is missing.

At any rate, he's my man for now, but I really don't see him being my man for forever.

"Mama, I found your other shoe," Jazzmine announced triumphantly, holding up a brown penny loafer instead of the match to the other black pump that I was wearing.

I shook my head and chuckled when I noticed what she was holding. I started to open my mouth to tell my precious child that the shoe she held was older than she is and not the one that I was looking for, but decided not to. Instead, I glanced at the clock and saw that I had exactly 22 minutes to get Jazzmine dropped off by Ma-Me and get myself across town to my interview.

I pictured the reproachful look on Ms. Hudson, my ex-supervisor's, face when she informed me that she had to let me go from the bank because of my excessive tardiness, and I did what I had to do. I grabbed my baby's hand and the scuffed brown shoe with Abraham Lincoln's tarnished face sticking out of the leather opening, and raced out of the door.

Verse twenty: breathless

I walked through the double glass doors of Baker and Brewer Advertising and was immediately impressed. The firm was located on the ninth floor of One Shell Square, the tallest building in New Orleans. The building was old, but well maintained, and right on the outskirt of the historic French Quarters, so I knew that the company had to be paying top dollar to lease office space there.

The décor was under-stated, but eclectic and expensive looking. Whoever designed the office seemed to have been going for a global theme, because I spotted accessories and furniture from China to France, to Africa, strewn throughout the large lobby and down a narrow hallway that I guessed led to individual offices and conference rooms.

Yeah, I can definitely see myself working here, I thought, before a curly haired brunette greeted me and interrupted my thoughts.

"Welcome to Baker and Brewer. How may I help you?" she asked.

I could tell that she was not from New Orleans, or even the United States, for that matter, because of her thick, hard to identify, foreign accent.

"Good morning. My name is Tracey Dubois. I'm here to interview for the receptionist position."

"Hello, Tracey," she smiled with teeth that looked as if they had been recently whitened. "Have a seat. Mr. Baker will see you shortly."

"Thank you," I murmured, wondering how beige my teeth looked in comparison to her light-brights.

Taking a seat in an antique looking chair with rolled gold arms and an upholstered back, I reminded myself how important it was for me to ace this job interview and nab myself a full-time J.O.B.

I couldn't think of the last time that I had extra money for luxuries such as teeth whitening or even a professional haircut. Hell, my last trip to a stylist was the week before; when I was first in line for a cosmetology student at Moler Beauty College. Thank goodness Shelly, my stylist in training, knew what she was doing. By the time she was finished, my ten-dollar haircut had me looking like a million bucks.

"Mr. Baker, Tracey Dubois is here to meet you," the young lady at the front desk announced through an intercom system.

"Uh, thanks Mitra. I'll be out in a minute," a sexy sounding male voice responded, which to my dismay, sounded like he had no idea of who I was or what I was there for. I smoothed down the skirt of my gray 'interview suit' and hoped that he sounded confused because her thick accent made my name sound like Gracie instead of Tracey and not because he had no intention of hiring me for the job.

I smelled him before I saw him. A masculine scent, with traces of sandalwood and coconut oil. What can I say? I know my scents, especially when it was a delicious smelling male scent. I could tell by just one whiff that he hadn't picked it up in Walgreens next to gallon sized bottles of Brute or Old Spice.

I've always been a sucker for men's cologne. There is just something about a man, smelling like a man that gets my juices flowing. By the time his body caught up with his scent, I found myself wondering, Carson *who*?

I took him in from bottom to top. Brown leather Ferragamo shoes, tan linen, perfectly tailored suit framing a narrow waist and broad shoulders, crisp white shirt with a tan and aqua colored tie. Damn!

Like Carson, he appeared older than me. Probably in his mid to late thirties, but he wore every year of it extremely well. He was a little over 6 feet tall, with medium brown, smooth as silk skin and full juicy lips that looked ripe and ready for sucking.

Oh Lord, I thought, as I tried to scooch my ugly penny loafers further underneath the Queen Anne chair. *I think I might be in trouble!*

Verse twenty-one: you put a move on my heart

"Baker and Brewer," I sang into the phone.
It was my second week on the job and I was finally getting the hang of their elaborate phone system. I took a deep breath and sank lower into the plush black leather office chair, pleased with myself for finally patching a caller through to their intended location.

"Yay, you did it!" Mitra exclaimed, raising her hand to give me a high five. Mitra was a serious high fiver. Everything that I did, no matter how big or small, warranted a high five from her. 'Yay, you answered the phone!' *High five.* 'Good job, you typed a memo!' *High five.* I'm gonna have to let her know that I'm not down for all that damn palm slapping, but she is so sweet and has been so helpful, that for now I guess I'll play along.

Mitra Qasimi is a 27-year-old immigrant from Dubai who found her way to the U.S. via London, then Amsterdam, then Egypt; following behind an American anthropology student. She is as sweet as she wants to be, but I didn't have the time or the desire to make any new friends. I liked her as a person, but I wished that she would stop inviting me to go shopping or club hopping with her after work.

Maybe it was a result of my experience with Val, but whatever it was, Mitra needed to understand that our friendship wasn't going any further than the four walls of our office.

Being a single parent usually left me brown bagging it more days than not. This particular morning was no different than most others, so after declining Mitra's offer to grab a bowl of gumbo and a shrimp sandwich from Mandina's, I headed to the small kitchenette to heat up my leftover lasagna.

I was just about to stuff the first forkful into my mouth when I heard Mr. Baker paging me over the intercom. I hastily covered my lunch with the top of my Tupperware container and nervously sauntered to my boss' office.

Baker and Brewer was a relatively small company that was just beginning to establish themselves among the major players in Louisiana's advertising community, so there was only four of us working in the office. Mitra served as the secretary and sometimes copy clerk. My role as receptionist was to answer the phones and greet incoming clients, and of course, Jaylen Baker and Byron Brewer were the HNICs: Head Negroes in Charge.

Even though I'd been with the company for over two weeks I hadn't had much face time with my fantastic looking boss. The company was in the midst of snagging a big account with Kirschman's, a Louisiana based furniture company that was looking to expand their business nationally, so Mr. Baker was spending a huge amount of time out of the office or held up inside the conference room.

I once caught a glance of the back of his head through a partially opened door, and I could hear his sexy voice as he dictated correspondence to Mitra, but it was never enough for me.

I knew that I had no business feeling this way, but for some reason I could not seem to stop thinking and fantasizing about my new boss. I guess it didn't help that his fragrance was always there, permeating every inch of the office. But I have to say that I was disappointed that we weren't working more closely together.

I lightly tapped on his office door and my heart fluttered as I heard his deep voice respond, "Come in. It's open."

This is crazy, I thought. I barely know this man. It felt unreal the effect he was having on me.

"Hi, Mr. Baker, you wanted to see me?" I asked, trying to act like it wasn't taking every ounce of my willpower not to run over and plop myself down on his lap.

"Yes, Tracey, come in and have a seat," he said, beaming across the room at me. "And please, call me Jaylen."

His smile was so infectious that I grinned back at him like a fool. I sat down and glanced around the office. It was my first time being invited into his private sanctum, and I was impressed with the dark mahogany of the desk and bookshelves and the bold, rich colors in the Oriental rug and chair upholstery. It seemed that everything about Jaylen Baker screamed class.

"So, how's it going?" he asked, looking at me like he was really interested in hearing my answer to his question.

"It's going well," I paused and then continued. "It took me a while to get the hang of the phone system, but now I think I have it under control. Mitra's been great. She has really taken the time to teach me the ropes. Any question that I have, she is always right there, ready and willing to answer them."

What in the hell is wrong with me? Why am I rambling on and on like some kind of moron? This man was probably asking me a rhetorical question. He is not interested in hearing about my dumb behind finally learning how to answer the telephone.

"Well, good. I'm glad that everything is going okay. And you're right, Mitra is the best. I don't know what we'd do without her around here. There have been many days that she's helped me out and saved my butt," he replied, smiling at me with that smile.

Dang, now he got me thinking about his butt.

I couldn't help wondering what he looked like outside of those designer suits.

I lost myself for a minute, as I sat there daydreaming about his butt, looking and feeling like a juicy, brown...

And then the most embarrassing thing happened. My stomach growled! Loud! I mean, very loud. Not some cute, little soft grrr, but a big, loud lion's growl. I wanted to crawl under that expensive Oriental rug and die!

Jaylen started laughing. He had a sexy, baritone laugh that immediately made you want to join in on the joke, even when the joke was on you.

"I'm sorry," he apologized. "It's time for your lunch, isn't it?"

"No...Yes... It's okay," I stammered.

"No, it's not okay. You're hungry and I'm sitting here wasting your time with chit-chat."

"You're not wasting my time," I insisted. "I've enjoyed talking to you. I think it's nice that you took the time out of your busy schedule to find out how I'm doing."

"Well, my schedule is not so busy that I'd let an employee starve to death," he chuckled. "How about joining me for lunch?"

"I, well, uh," I stammered. I wanted to give myself a Stooges style slap across the face so I could pull myself together. "No, you don't have to do that," I finally managed.

"Are you sure?" he asked. "I'm going to Deanie's and they have the best seafood platters in the entire city."

I hesitated for a second and then took a quick glance at his ring finger, which was occupied by a simple platinum band. I knew that being alone with this man was not a good idea. *He* may have thought that he was simply rescuing a ravished employee, but *I knew* that what I really had in mind was ravishing him!

"No, I'd better not. I have something that I need to wrap up around here. And besides, I brought my world-famous lasagna for lunch."

"World famous, huh?" he kidded. "Fantastic on phones and she can cook too? It seems like I've hit the jackpot."

Wait a minute. Was he flirting with me? Keep it up, Mr. Jaylen Baker, and you really might hit the jackpot! I thought as I sashayed out of his office.

Verse twenty-two: going in circles

It was an unusually brisk fall day for early October in New Orleans. Crunchy brown and orange leaves swirled around our feet as Carson and I strolled through the French Quarters, enjoying the sights and sounds of the city.

We took a romantic carriage ride through Jackson Square and then pigged out on a calorie filled breakfast of beignets and Café au Laits. I normally counted every calorie that passed through my lips but today I was willing to risk a layer of extra padding on the hips in order to spend some uninterrupted quality time with Carson. With my new job at the advertising firm, twice a week gigs at Harrah's, and Carson's demanding schedule at the hospital, we were both beginning to feel a disconnect between us. And to be honest, I was beginning to feel uncomfortable about the amount of time that I was spending thinking and daydreaming about my new boss.

We decided to do the tourist thing and stroll down St. Peters to Bourbon Street. Even though it was barely 10:00 in the morning, there were already dozens of people walking the streets of the Quarters, drinking hard and partying harder.

We couldn't help but shake our heads at the group of people walking in front of us. The guys were holding Mardi Gras beads high over their heads while the young ladies were swiping at and begging for them as if they were solid gold instead of worthless, plastic baubles.

Carson chuckled and said, "I guess that just goes to show that ignorance comes in every color. Everybody thinks that it's the brothers out here acting crazy in the Quarters, but look around you, white folks are out here early in the morning, drunk and acting wild and crazy just like everyone else."

Something about Carson's comment bothered me. I guess it was because there are times when he acts so bougie and critical of people that I can't help but wonder if he is mentally judging me. I realized that I was probably being overly sensitive; especially since I've been known to turn up my nose at wild and raunchy behavior myself, but something about that statement coming from Carson's lips rubbed me the wrong way.

Maybe it's because he's an outsider, from Newport News, Virginia, and had "buddies" named Skip and Tom. He is always so straight arrow and by the book that I can't even picture him letting loose and acting crazy over something as silly as a strand of beads.

I shook my head and tried to toss aside any negative thoughts that I was having of Carson. I wasn't stupid. I knew that he was a catch by any measure, and I was lucky to have him in my life. A young, handsome, soon-to-be rich doctor was interested in taking care of me and my daughter. Why couldn't I just get with the program and make myself fall in love with him? Why did I have to notice the dorky looking short sleeve dress shirt with the red and blue striped Walmart tie that he was wearing? Or the fact that he ate his beignets with a knife and fork instead of diving into the pile of powdered sugar confection as most people would do? Why did I keep comparing him to Jaylen, and why did he continue to come up short?

Later that afternoon, Carson dropped me off at mama's house so that I could relieve Ma-Me from babysitting duties and join everyone for our traditional, first of the month family brunch.

When I walked through the door, Ma-Me was in her house coat and sitting on the living room couch, rolling her knee-high stockings down her pudgy shins. When she noticed me standing there, she shot me one of her infamous looks, and I knew that she was about to jump on my case about missing church again and about the amount of time I spent away from Jazzmine.

I cut her off at the pass by giving her a kiss on the cheek and presenting her with a Mother of Pearl decorated hair comb that I picked up at a little boutique in the French Quarters.

Ma-Me was uncomfortable with displays of affection, unless they were coming from Jazz, the joy of her life, so she just muttered, "Hmpff," grabbed her gift and shuffled out of the room. She thought that I didn't see it, but I caught the corner of a smile on her face before she left.

Whatever we were doing, wherever we were at, we Dubois tried our best to congregate on the first Sunday of every month. Most Sundays we would meet up at mama's house and drive to church together, but ever since I got pregnant with Jazz, I found myself using any and every excuse that I could think of to get out of going to Mount Zion. No one knew for sure that JP was Jazzmine's father, but most took one look at her sandy colored curls and her butterscotch colored complexion and they knew. What they didn't know was the circumstances of her conception. And that was a secret that I intended to take to my grave.

Even mama didn't know for sure that JP was Jazzmine's father. Of course, she had her suspicions but I would never confirm nor deny them. I knew that it was frustrating for her, but I just couldn't bring myself to tell her the truth. And the reality of the situation was, she couldn't force me. I'd quickly come to realize that there was nothing that mama could do to me that was worse than what had already been done.

Even though I did not feel like hearing it, especially on such a beautiful day, I knew Ma-Me was right and that I needed to make some changes in my life and better balance my time between singing, working, my love life, and spending time with my daughter.

It wasn't that I was pleased with the amount of time that I spent away from Jazzmine, but what was I supposed to do? I was a single mother who had never received a dime of financial assistance from anyone. I knew that she and mama had good intentions and only wanted what is best for both Jazzmine as well as for me, but I was getting tired of them making me feel guilty when all I was trying to do was provide for my child. It wasn't like I was out in the clubs, shaking my behind and picking up any Joe Schmoe who offered me a drink. I was out there, working two jobs, trying to afford to give my child everything that she deserved. I knew that it was not an ideal situation, but it was simply easier to have Jazz spend the weekdays with Ma-Me and I pick her up every Friday after work.

It wasn't ideal, but it was all I could come up with at the time.

Verse twenty-three: whatever happens

The Audubon Room at Harrah's Casino smelled of stale cigarettes and weak alcohol and was filled with aging men dreaming of comebacks on the poker tables, housewives recovering from slot machine induced carpal tunnel, and tourists itching at the bit to get back to the outrageousness of the French Quarters.

I'd been the headlining act at the club for over a year and I was sadly beginning to realize that the big break that I was waiting for was unlikely to come walking through those doors.

Nonetheless, I needed the job to help pay the bills; and singing, even for less than enthusiastic crowds, still brought me the kind of joy that I was unable to find anywhere else. So, there I was, closing out my set with a personal favorite, Whitney Houston's *Saving All My Love for You,* when I looked out into the audience and straight into the dark brown eyes of Mr. Jaylen Baker.

I'd been singing for so many years that I rarely get nervous when singing in front of family and friends, but when my eyes met Jaylen's eyes, and he smiled his mischievous little half smile at me, the butterflies in my stomach took flight, and for a second I couldn't even remember what song I was supposed to be performing.

Then I thought about the countless times that I'd made a fool of myself in front of this man; the stupid brown penny loafers and my stomach growling louder than the Lion King, and I willed myself to get it together.

I knew that I was looking good in my skintight black jeans and bright yellow sequenced tank top so I grabbed the microphone from its stand, sashayed across the stage and began working the audience. A middle-aged man with bad psoriasis was sitting up front, eying me down like I was the jackpot that he planned on hitting, so I focused my attention on him, all the while pretending that he was Jaylen.

The Whitney Houston tune was supposed to be my last song, but I was too nervous to leave the stage and find out what Jaylen was doing there, so I cued the band up to play Vanessa William's *Whatever Happens.* I figured that song to be fitting because I knew that whatever happened between us from this point on was totally out of my control.

I knew there was no more putting it off, so I gave Tyrone and Terry, my drummer and bassist, a pound, said, "peace out" to Sean and DeWayne, the pianist and guitarist, then I smoothed down my bob and walked over to the bar. I sat on the stool next to Jaylen, but instead of acknowledging him, I sat with my back to him and ordered a rum punch.

"Busy night, huh?" I asked, attempting to make small talk with the new bartender, whose name I had already forgotten, even though he'd introduced himself to me not even two hours earlier.

"Yeah, pretty much," he agreed.

About two minutes later, right around the time when I'd run out of small talk with George, which the bartender reminded me was his name, Jaylen asked, "So, what did you think about that singer? Pretty bad, huh?"

"Aww, she wasn't too bad," I replied with a straight face. "I mean, she's no Aretha Franklin or Patti LaBelle, but I guess she'll do in a pinch."

"Yeah, in a pinch I guess I'd listen to her again. Actually, after about my fourth drink she didn't sound half bad," he teased.

"Alright you," I laughed, lightly punching him on the arm, which was as hard as granite, I might add. "What are you doing here, anyway? And why are you sitting here all by yourself?"

"I don't know. This will probably sound crazy to you," he began, and then stopped speaking.

"What may sound crazy?" I asked, feeling puzzled, wondering if there was any way that he could possibly be feeling the same things that I was feeling.

"There is just something about you," he went on. "Every time I look at you, I keep getting this weird sense of de ja vu; as if I've seen you or met you before. I couldn't shake the feeling, so I finally pried some information about you out of Mitra."

I looked at him with my mouth hanging open.

"Really? And what kind of information about me did Mitra give you?"

"Not much. Apparently, you're as guarded with her about your personal life as you are with the rest of us."

I started laughing at his statement. "You think I'm guarded?" I asked. "If you think that I'm guarded then you really don't know anything about me. I'm as far away from guarded as a person can be. My life is an open book. And to be honest, the story is really not that fascinating."

"I find that hard to believe," he said, looking deeply into my eyes. "Take tonight, for instance. Mitra told me that you sing here a few nights a week, but I had no idea that you could sing like that! Damn girl, you sound amazing! That jazz set you did was insane! What are you doing working for us? You should be singing professionally."

I blushed about a million shades of magenta before responding.

"A girl has to pay the bills some way," I joked. "At least until Jimmy Jam and Terry Lewis come a' callin'."

"Well, with a voice like that, they'll be calling soon," he said, looking at me with those eyes, smiling at me with those lips.

"Anyway," he said, breaking our stare, "I'd better be getting home. I just wanted to see where you were moonlighting on us at, and now I know. Baker and Brewer had better start looking for a new receptionist soon. I have a feeling that you'll be on to bigger and better things before we know it."

I can't think of anything bigger or better, I thought, staring him down, trying to drink in every ounce of him.

He stood up, slipped on his navy suit jacket, and bent to kiss me on the cheek.

"I'll see you in the morning, Miss Dubois," he said.

"Not if I see you first, Mr. Baker," I replied.

Dang, did I just say that lame ass line out loud?

Somehow, I'd managed to make a fool out of myself yet again.

Verse twenty-four: she works hard for the money

We all had our roles at the office. I guess, according to Jaylen, I was the talented, mysterious one. Mitra was the flighty one, known for outlandish acts such as highlighting her hair purple, going on an all soup diet, or deciding to write a self-help book for Persian girls dating American guys.

Jaylen was the calm, cool and collected one. I'd never seen him break a sweat, not even when the printer screwed up a huge job and it looked like we were going to lose out on the Kirschman's account. He simply picked up the phone, spoke to someone on the other end with that sexy, yet demanding voice, and within fifteen minutes everything was taken care of.

Byron Brewer, the other boss man at Baker and Brewer, was a perpetual harried mess. He zipped into the office most mornings with his clothes disheveled and his shoulder length dreads flying every which way, looking like he's forgotten which way was up. And by lunch time he was usually a frenzied fool.

I knew that part of his problem was the way that he guzzled that strong ass Starbucks coffee as if it was going out of style, but other than that I think that he just needed to take a chill pill. And this morning, the way he ran around the office, barking out orders and making demands, I was tempted to slip that magic pill into his double Grande mocha latte my damn self.

Though he drove me crazy at times, for the most part, I could feel where he was coming from. According to Mitra, Byron grew up the poor middle child of nine children. Everyone assumed he would do the same as most young, black boys growing up in the Calliope projects; turn out to be one of the three D's: drug dealer, dead, or a do-nothing for my kid's baby-daddy.

Byron fooled them, though. He had skills on the basketball court as well as having lofty dreams. He used his balling to get him a scholarship to Morehouse College in Atlanta. Once he was there, he used his brains to scheme his way out of the streets.

His roommate, marketing major, Jaylen Baker, also dreamed of a better life. While most college seniors were out partying and trying to squeeze the last little drop of fun in before their real lives began, Jaylen and Byron were up long hours of the night; visualizing, planning, and even praying for The Baker and Brewer Advertising firm.

So yeah, being the person that I am: a single mother and aspiring artist, on most days I totally understand his sense of urgency. I'm sure that he wakes up most mornings thinking about his long road to success, and the quick shortcut that could take him right back to the Calliope.

Mitra waltzed into the office shortly after Byron and I arrived, wearing a short black dress and four-inch green leather pumps, looking like she didn't have a care in the world; even though she was almost twenty minutes late for work.

"Good afternoon," I joked, but she just flicked her wrist at me and shrugged it off.

"Please," she said with her cute sounding accent, "as late as I stay here most nights, who cares if I'm a few minutes late in the morning." Then she added, "When I'm here, I'm here."

"It's cool with me," I responded, wanting her to know that I was only teasing her and I couldn't care less what time she came or went. "And it seems to be cool with the guys. I've never heard them complain about your schedule."

"Yeah, they're fantastic," she affirmed, putting her purse into her desk drawer and sitting behind her desk. "I really lucked up when I found this job. My last boss was a fuck."

I laughed to myself because Mitra was always trying to curse or use some type of slang and it always came out sounding hilarious. Between her accent, and her not really knowing how to properly curse (the way she would have had she grown up around mama and Ma-Me), instead of angering or intimidating her intended verbal lashing target, she usually just left them chuckling and shaking their heads at her.

"So, how did you come to work for Jaylen and Byron?" I asked.

I was dying to press her for information about Jaylen, but I didn't want to seem so obvious. After our chat at the casino the previous night I was more confused, and more intrigued, by him than ever.

"I was actually working for a law firm that handled all the company's incorporation work when they were just getting started," she answered. "I spent a lot of time with the guys, ironing out some small legal issues, and we just clicked. I was unhappy at the law firm, and when Jaylen offered me a job here, even though it was for less money, I jumped at the chance."

"Dang, y'all must have really hit it off if you were willing to work for less money," I said, thinking about the fact that every one of my nickels counted, which would never leave me with the luxury of choosing to work for less money, no matter how good my new boss smelled.

"Are you kidding? I would have probably taken the job for free just to get a whiff of Jaylen every day. Have you smelled that guy? He smells incredible! And he looks even better!"

Mitra sounded like she had been roaming around the inside of my mind. Her comments about Jaylen made me uncomfortable, though, and made me wonder if Mr. Baker was spoken for more than once.

Verse twenty-five: after the love has lost its shine

The drip from the kitchen faucet was driving me a special kind of mad, but I didn't, for the life of me, have the strength to get up and turn it off. I was sitting at my kitchen table, in a state of disbelief. Carson just left and we'd decided that we needed to take a break from one another. Actually, *he* decided, and those were the exact words that he used.

"Tracey, I can feel some discontentment from you, and to be perfectly honest, I must say that I am feeling unfulfilled in this relationship as well. I think that in order to figure out what we both want we should probably take a break from one another."

I almost choked on the root beer that I was drinking. My nostrils started burning as the drink threatened to come out of my nose. I hadn't seen that coming. I knew that I wasn't exactly gung-ho about our relationship, but I had no idea that Carson was feeling the same way.

I sat there, stunned and silent. He was right, but I couldn't speak because I had too many thoughts going on inside my head at the same time. I was sad because Carson really is a great guy and I knew that on some level I was going to miss him. On the other hand, I was also relieved because I knew that I didn't feel for him the way I needed to in order to have a lasting, loving relationship. But I didn't want to hurt him by telling him that, for me at least, he wasn't the one. And honestly, I was sitting there thinking to myself, who in the hell says things like 'feeling discontentment and unfulfilled.' If he hadn't caught me so off guard, I would have laughed in his face. He must have been coached on how to break up with me by Skip and Tom.

After a while I got up to grab another soda from the fridge and make myself a grilled cheese sandwich. The butter had just started browning in my skillet when the phone rang. I placed my sandwich onto the griddle, lightly flattened it down with a spatula, and reached for my cordless phone.

"Mama, where are you? I thought you were coming to pick me up."

Jazzmine's sweet little voice on the other end of the line made me smile, but then I felt guilty for letting her stay over with Ma-Me and not picking her up the night before like I had promised. I couldn't help but remember the countless nights that Lynette and I stayed up waiting for mama to come and get us when she told us that she would.

"I'm sorry, Pudding Pop," I said. "I worked late last night and when I called Ma-Me to tell her that I was on my way to pick you up and she told me that you had already fallen asleep."

"Oh," Jazz said slowly, seeming to turn my excuse around in her mind to decide if she was buying it. "Okay, she finally lamented. "But next time, come anyway. I wanted to wake up in my own bed."

"Yes, m'am." I laughed at the fact that my four-year-old daughter was giving me orders and telling me what to do.

"Come now, mama," she continued. "I have something that I want to tell you."

"I'll be there in a little while, but you can tell me your big news now."

"Nope, I can't. I want to tell your face."

"Okay, Pumpkin Pie," I laughed. "I'll be there in a few minutes so you can tell my face."

I hung up the phone and wondered when I had become the type of parent that calls their child every sweet-sounding name under the sun. I also wondered how it was that Jazzmine could always cheer me up, no matter what I was going through.

And then I remembered my grilled cheese sandwich, which was looking more blackened than grilled. I turned the burner off, threw the cheesy mess into the trashcan, and left to pick up my daughter.

Jazzmine couldn't wait to tell my face her exciting news. She had been chosen to sing a solo in the church's Sunbeam Choir, and she was excited beyond belief. She had been walking around the apartment for hours, singing snatches of her song before I was finally able to quiet her down by making her a turkey sandwich and turning The Mickey Mouse Club on the television.

I was just about to settle myself down and enjoy the solitude when I heard a loud knock at my door. For a minute I considered not answering. I had been looking forward to an evening with just Jazzmine and I chilling out together with no interruptions, but then I thought that it might have been Carson, reconsidering and wanting to give out relationship another shot. I'm not gonna lie, I was a little disappointed when I opened the door and saw that it wasn't Carson, coming back hat in hand, but rather Essence, whom I had been keeping in touch with over the phone but hadn't seen in person for the better part of a year.

Essence was standing on my doorstep in a white, two sizes too small halter dress, with her breasts hanging so low that they looked like cow udders.

"Got milk?" I joked, but she missed my attempt at comedy and walked right past me.

"No, I ain't got no damn milk, but I sure hope you got some Alize up in this bitch," she responded.

"Essence, what did I tell you about coming to my house acting all ghetto? Lower your voice and watch your language," I admonished. "Jazzmine is in the other room watching cartoons."

"Oh, I'm sorry." Essence started whispering as if she was in church, which is a place that she made a point of going to only three times a year: Christmas, Easter, and Mother's Day.

"You don't have to whisper, nutcase," I teased. "I said that she was watching cartoons, not that she was in there studying for the bar exam."

Essence started laughing and raised her voice a smidgen. "Girl, I'm trippin'. You know I don't know how to act. Hey Jazzmine, baby. Come give Auntie Essence a hug," she yelled.

"And you..." she pointed at me with camouflage colored acrylic nails. "Since you mentioned the word bar, get your skinny ass over there and pour my drink. I got some news to tell you!"

After I poured Essence a water glass filled with White Zinfandel, which was all I had in the apartment, she spilled what she had come over to tell me.

Patrice was getting married.

I wasn't terribly surprised by the news. Out of all my girls from L9, Patrice was the one who was the most settled and goal oriented. After the group broke up, Patrice enrolled in cosmetology school. She started off doing braids in the back of her grandmother's kitchen and wound up, only three years later, with an extremely successful hair and nail shop on Magazine Street.

So no, finding out that Patrice had settled down and was about to be married is not what surprised me. What surprised me was the name that Essence uttered when she mentioned the groom-to-be. Patrice was marrying Cat Man Simms, one of the biggest drug dealers in New Orleans.

"Please tell me you're joking," I begged when Essence gave me the news.

"No girl, I'm serious as a heart attack. That trick was able to pin down Mr. Big Time himself."

"Wow," I said, but couldn't think of anything to back it up with, so I left that one flimsy word floating in the wind.

"Anyway, that's not even the best part," Essence continued rambling. "The best part is that Cat Man

104

heard a copy of the demo that we put together beaucoup years ago and he wants us to cut another joint. He says he's gon' bankroll the whole thing."

I started shaking my head before she even got half of her sentence out.

"Nope, nope, nope... I am not interested. I am a mother now, Essence. I can't be running all over town with y'all, singing for peanuts. Besides, I would never trust my career, and probably even my life, to Cat Man Simms!"

Essence looked at me as if I'd lost my natural born mind.

"Tracey, what you bugging out for? Do you realize the props that Cat Man gets in this city? He ain't about to let nothing happen to us? And do you know how much money that dude got? We ain't 'bout to be singing for no damn peanuts! This shit 'bout to go down smoother than Peter Pan Peanut Butter."

Essence started cracking up laughing at her own joke. I had to admit, it was sort of funny, so I chuckled along with her.

I was serious, though. My days of chasing that dream were over. I poured us each another glass of wine, we spent a few more minutes discussing Patrice's upcoming nuptials and then I said goodbye to my friend for the last time.

Verse twenty-six: ladies night

Finding street parking in the Quarters was almost as impossible as winning the Powerball, so when I noticed an empty spot on North Rampart Street I swerved my ride into the tight fit and declared myself a winner. I checked my hair and lipstick in my rearview mirror and began making my way up Frenchmen Street, ready to meet my girls for dinner.

By the time I made it to The Praline Connection there was already a line snaking through the door and wrapped outside of the restaurant. I wasn't surprised. Tourists got a kick out of the waiters walking around in their black felt hats and their over-dramatic Cajun accents and locals frequented the spot because of the occasional live music, and of course the slamming food.

My eyes did a quick sweep and then I saw Lynette and Kenya waving their arms, trying to get my attention. I made my way through the crowd and gave them both huge hugs. It felt like forever since we'd last gotten together.

"Oh my gosh, Tootie, look at you!" I gushed, staring up at my little sister. Though she was younger than me, Lynette was at least four inches taller. I took in her casual outfit of skin tight True Religion jeans, a cream colored fitted tee shirt, and about twenty gold bangles traveling up her arm, and couldn't help wondering when did my little sister, with the two ponytails and missing front teeth, grow into this stunning beauty with flawless, caramel colored skin, lightly highlighted with Bobbi Brown makeup and Mac lip gloss.

"Hey Fruity, you look great too," she said, throwing my own embarrassing nickname back at me.

"And look at you!" I said, reaching over and hugging Kenya again. "What are you trying to do, disappear on us?"

Kenya has always been a little on the "fluffy side" as she liked to call it. Every time I looked around, she was starting some new diet or exercise plan, but this latest one looked like it was actually working. Kenya was at least fifteen pounds lighter than she was the last time I saw her and she looked better than ever.

"Nope," Kenya joked, "Not trying to disappear, I'm trying to be seen... just like you and sister long legs over here."

Thirty minutes later we were finally being seated. We followed Pete, our host, to a table in the center of the restaurant and wasted no time filling each other in on the crazy goings on in our lives. After listening to Lynette and Kenya gripe about academic life—they were both finishing up their last year of

107

college I filled them in on my breakup with Carson and began regaling them with tales from the work front.

"So far so good," I answered in response to Lynette's question about how everything was going at Baker and Brewer. "Everyone seems nice enough. The pay isn't great but it's better than what I was making at the bank."

"That's great," Kenya said. "What about Harrah's. Have you been able to pick up those extra shows that you were telling me about?"

"No, not yet," I admitted. "Don't get me wrong, I am forever grateful to Uncle Mervin for hooking me up with the gig, but Joe, my supervisor at Harrah's has got to be biggest slimeball in the world."

"Really? What does he do?" They both wanted to know.

"He keeps dangling the notion of my doing more shows and making more money in my face, but then it's always followed up with some unspoken favor that I'll eventually have to do for him. Can you believe that jerk even had the nerve to use the phrase 'you scratch my back and I'll scratch yours?'"

"Are you serious? What a pervert!" Kenya said.

"Yeah, I know. Don't worry, though. I know how to handle the likes of him. Believe me; I get enough practice trying to fend off those drunken fools around the casino." And then I wistfully added, "Too bad he can't be more like Jaylen."

Their ears perked up as if they were vultures listening out for prey. Finally, Lynette asked the question that was on the tip of both of their tongues, "Jaylen? Who is this Jaylen that you are practically swooning over?"

"I'm not swooning," I laughed. "Who does that, anyway—swoon? I'm simply saying that my boss at Baker and Brewer is so much easier to work under, that's all."

"Yeah, I bet you'd like to work under him," Kenya mumbled under her breath, all innocent like, and took a swig of her lemon water. I swatted at her and she started giggling at her crude little joke.

And then Lynette threw in for good measure, "And since when did you start calling your boss by his first name?

"I started when he asked me to," I said. "And that's enough," I insisted. I could feel my face turning red. I must be the most blushing'ist black girl in the world. Geez.

"He's my boss, that's all. My very married boss! I'm just saying that he's a nice guy, that's all!"

Thank goodness our entrees arrived at that moment, saving me from having to further defend my feelings towards Jaylen.

I dove into my soft-shell crab as if I hadn't eaten in a week.

Verse twenty-seven: if only for one night

Rain was pouring down in buckets and the biting wind caused my three-dollar umbrella to turn inside out, resulting in me arriving at work looking like a five-dollar fool.

I formulated a quick plan to sneak through the doors and make a hasty retreat to the restroom so I could dry off and make myself more presentable. But of course, things never seemed to go my way, at least not when it came to me impressing Jaylen.

As soon as I entered the office, I noticed that Jaylen, Byron, and Mitra were all in the conference room, laughing and talking animatedly. I tried tip-toeing past them, but Byron noticed me and motioned me over.

I laughed, despite my disheveled appearance, when I saw them because they were in there celebrating up a storm, drinking mimosas and more than halfway on their way to tipsy at eight o'clock in the morning.

The fellas had just found out that they had landed the Kirschman's account, which would go a long way towards establishing their business and even put them in a different, more impressive, tax bracket. I was extremely proud of them, and picked up a champagne flute without having to be told twice.

By the time lunch time rolled around, we hadn't gotten a lick of work done. We were sitting around, patting ourselves on the back and brainstorming ways to make the company stronger.

I guess that was the good thing about working for a small company. It really felt like a family affair, and their success, in a way, felt like mine. By the end of the day we'd all decided that the party wasn't over. The plan was, we would go home, get cleaned and jazzied up, and meet one another at The G Spot, a new restaurant that had just opened downtown and was getting rave reviews by the locals as well as the food critics.

Before continuing the celebration, I needed to first run by mama's house and deliver a Happy Meal and a kiss to Jazzmine. After listening to about fifteen minutes of Ma-Me griping about my leaving Jazz to spend the night yet again, I was able to make a quick departure as soon as she turned her back to answer the phone. Then I jetted home to change into the little black dress that I had been saving for a special occasion. I couldn't think of an occasion more special than I planned on making this one.

I put Jill Scott in my CD player and generously poured vanilla scented bubble bath into the tub. After sudsing up and harmonizing along with Jilly from Philly long enough for my fingers to turn to prunes, I then lotioned every part of my body that I could reach with some smell good that I had just picked up from Victoria's Secret and daydreamed that Jaylen was lotioning and massaging those parts that I could not reach.

I slid on my black dress, slipped into strappy black sandals, and once I was convinced that I was slammin' from head to toe, I grabbed my purse and headed towards a night that I was sure that I wouldn't forget.

By the time I pulled up in front of The G Spot our party was already seated and working on their second round of Hurricanes. It crossed my mind as I was driving over that the gang may have decided to bring their significant others to celebrate with us.

In particular, Jaylen may have decided to bring his wife, which I'm ashamed to admit, made me as jealous as all get out. But I was pleased to see, once I got there, that they were all flying solo, just like me.

"What's up, my people?" I asked as I plopped down in the empty seat next to Byron and motioned to the waiter to bring me a glass of whatever the others were drinking. I couldn't help noticing how close Mitra was sitting next to Jaylen and it made me again wonder if they had something going on. Then I had to remind myself, for about the millionth time, that the man was married and it didn't matter who he was sitting next to, he would never have anything going on with me.

"Tracey D!" Byron bellowed into my ear as he slung an arm across my shoulder. "Glad to see you finally decided to show your face in the place!"

"Yep, I finally made it. Glad to see that you guys decided to wait for me," I kidded.

"Sorry dude, the party waits for no one," Byron countered, and slurped an oyster into his mouth.

"Well, I guess I need to catch up, then," I said, taking a swig from my glass, and reaching towards the tray of appetizers.

About two hours, and countless drinks, later we were still sitting at our table, full as ticks and making no moves to leave anytime soon. I couldn't remember the last time I'd had such a good time. Jaylen and Byron encouraged us to order a little of everything, so we pretty much ate off one another's plates and sampled almost the entire menu. The food was off the charts, and that's saying a lot because we New Orleanians considered our food an art form and practically a religion.

Before we knew it, we looked around and the restaurant was practically empty. I glanced over at our waiter and noticed that he was glaring impatiently at us, probably hoping that we'd hurry and leave so he could tally up his tips and carry his butt home.

It seemed that Byron and I made eye contact with the waiter at the exact same time. By then, Byron had traveled long past tipsy and was knocking on needing a designated driver's door, so it didn't take much to piss him off.

"What the hell is that fun boy looking at?" he slurred, ridiculing the guy's tight black pants and girlish manner.

"Chill out, man," Jaylen warned. "And lower your voice. I'm sure that Tracey is tired of you yelling in her ear all night," he said, and then winked at me.

He winked at me! What the heck does that mean? Was he, or was he not, flirting with me? Lord, I wished that I was better at reading this man.

"Chill out, my ass!" Byron barked. "I done spent a grip in this restaurant and I don't appreciate this faggot trying to rush me out of here!"

Jaylen was about to say something else to try to diffuse the situation, but before he could utter another word, a good-looking guy, who appeared to be in charge, was standing at our table.

"Is everything okay over here?" he asked with a smile on his face, but I could tell that his antenna was up and he was prepared to turn up the heat if he needed to.

"Yes. Everything is fine. Your restaurant is very nice," Mitra said, attempting to dazzle him with her smile.

"Yes, the food was amazing," I piped in, hoping that our enjoyable night out wasn't about to turn into an embarrassing scene of us being thrown out of one of the hottest restaurants in the city.

"Good, I'm glad that y'all enjoyed yourselves," he said, while looking at me so long and intensely that I was beginning to feel uncomfortable. Just when I was about to say something to break up the tension he asked, "Is your name, Tracey Dubois?"

I figured that he must have seen me perform at Harrah's, so I simply shook my head yes and began to turn my body to dismiss him. But he grabbed my hand and pulled me out of my seat and into a big bear hug.

"Oh my God, girl! How have you been? You look fantastic! It's me, Greg!

Greg. Gregory Adams. The chubby little dude from church," he laughed, trying to get me to remember him.

Oh my gosh, I thought.

Of course, I remembered him. As soon as he said Gregory Adams, I knew who he was. I was just trying to match up the husky little nerd that I knew from Sunday School and the church choir with the handsome brother standing in front of me.

"Yes, of course I remember you, Greg. How are you?"

"Oh, I can't complain. Been keeping busy and trying to make things happen."

"So, you work here?" I asked.

"Actually, I own the place. I'm also the head chef, so I appreciate your compliment about the food."

I was about to congratulate Greg on owning such a well-run and successful restaurant, but Jaylen cut me off by loudly clearing his throat.

"So, are you going to introduce us to your friend?" Jaylen asked, sounding, dare I say it, a tad bit jealous.

I gave a little embarrassed chuckle when I looked down and saw that I was holding onto Greg in a kung-fu death grip. I released his arm and tried, unsuccessfully, to find a comfortable spot to place my hands. After flailing around for a couple of seconds, probably looking like a complete fool, I finally folded my arms in front of me before making the introductions.

"I'm sorry, guys. This is my good friend, Gregory. We practically grew up together," I said.

Hi'ya's and nice to meet you's were exchanged around the table and then, after another squeeze and a promise to keep in touch, Greg excused himself and disappeared back into the kitchen.

After a brief period of uncomfortable silence Mitra cleared the air by loudly proclaiming, "Wow, your chef friend is hot! And I'm sure you noticed that he wasn't wearing a ring. He sure seemed happy to see you!"

"Greg? Please...we know one another from way back," I quickly countered, and tried to change the subject. "Are you guys ready to call it a night?"

"Yeah, I guess we need to get out of here while we're ahead," Jaylen piped in. "B. man, you need a designated driver, so hand over the keys."

He reached his hand over the table, lightly brushing my arm in the process.

"Hell no, I'm not giving up my keys. I can drive, man. Ain't nothing wrong with me," Byron slurred.

"I know there is nothing wrong with you, sweetie," Mitra intervened. "But actually, I don't feel like driving home alone. Come on, drive home with me, will ya?"

He seemed to think about it for about a minute, and then he said, "Alright, I'll ride home with you. But only because you're fine, not because I can't drive myself home. So, don't think that you're tricking my ass."

Jaylen laughed and then said, "Good, then that's settled. We'll see you two tomorrow." And with that, they headed toward the valet stand.

Jaylen and I were left at the table together and I could feel my nerves returning. I took a good look at him, in a pair of black slacks and a black Ralph Lauren sweater and it took every ounce of my willpower to not throw myself into his arms.

Jaylen took care of the check and then we stood up to leave. He placed his hand on my lower back to escort me out of the restaurant, and I swear, I felt a current run through my body. My legs were weak.

I'm going to blame a combination of the alcohol and my hormones on my next move. Once we made our way out to the valet stand, I ignored my six-year-old Honda parked at a meter two blocks away and I pulled out my cell phone and pretended that I was calling someone to pick me up. Jaylen heard my end of the fictional conversation and offered to give me a ride home. Mission accomplished.

Verse twenty-eight: body and soul

The ride home was electric. The sexual tension seemed almost palpable in Jaylen's tiny two-seater Mercedes SLK and I felt positive that I wasn't the only one feeling it. At one point our fingers brushed against each other's as we both reached to adjust the air conditioner. Then, without thinking or talking about it, our fingers intertwined, and we rode the rest of the way to my apartment, silently holding hands.

By the time we pulled up to my complex I was unsure about how I wanted, or expected, the night to end. Even though I'd manipulated circumstances so that we would end up alone, now that I was actually in the moment, I was unsure of how to proceed.

After pulling into my parking spot, Jaylen disengaged his fingers from mine and leaned over and gave me a kiss on the corner of my lips.

I would have done practically anything to stay locked in that moment, but out of nowhere, I heard mama's voice whispering in my ear, "Don't start something that you don't plan on finishing...and don't you dare finish what you've already started."

I shook her words off and kissed Jaylen back. Then, against my better judgment I asked, "What are we doing?"

He thought about it for a second and then he said, "Carpe diem. Seizing the day."

I pulled away and looked him in his eyes. "Jaylen, don't give me a suave answer," I said. "Give me a real answer. What are we doing?

"Okay, fair enough... I'm not sure what we're doing," he admitted, though he continued pecking my lips and kissing up and down my neck.

Then he paused. "Tracey, you know that I am married, right?"

"Yes, of course I do," I answered, suddenly embarrassed, wondering if he was aware that my deception was the reason that we were sitting together at that moment.

I started babbling, "Look, I'm sorry if I've been forward tonight. I don't know what's come over me. This behavior is not really me. Can we just pretend that this never happened?"

"You have no need to apologize," he replied. "I should be the one apologizing to you." He'd stopped kissing my neck, but he was still holding onto me in a light embrace.

I reluctantly pulled away from him, unbuckled my seatbelt and moved to open the door. He placed his hand over mine to stop me.

"Are you alright? Are you upset with me?" he asked.

"Why should I be upset with you?" I countered. "You didn't do anything wrong. I'm just a little embarrassed, is all."

"You have no reason to be embarrassed. You are a sexy, beautiful woman, and don't think for one moment that I haven't thought about spending time with you, because I have. Tracey, I like you. I mean, really like you, and to be honest I have been having thoughts about you since you first walked through my door that I know that I have no business having. But the bottom line is, I made a commitment to someone else. My marriage isn't perfect, but I think that you deserve better that the 'my wife doesn't understand me' spiel."

"Yeah...okay...well, goodnight," I stammered. I was unsure how to respond to his statement and I just wanted to get out of that car and into the privacy of my house so that I could think, or cry, or both.

Somehow or another, I was able to make my way out of the car and up the walkway to my front door. I was dying to turn around and check the expression on Jaylen's face, just to make sure that I wasn't the only one in pain, but instead, I willed myself to stay strong and continue to walk away. I fumbled with the lock until I was finally able to get the door opened. And then I hurried and locked it behind me while I at least had a slight modicum of dignity left.

I kicked my sandals off, and the tears were just beginning to fall when I heard three light taps on the door. I pulled the door open, hoping against hope, and he was there, smiling that smile at me.

He stepped over the threshold and pulled me into his arms.

"I tried to leave, but I couldn't," he said.

"I tried to pretend that I didn't care, but I couldn't," I said, as he wiped the tears from my eyes.

Verse twenty-nine: the morning after

Work, the next day, felt surreal. I walked around the office feeling awkward and exposed, wondering if my co-workers could take one look at me and know that I'd spent the better part of the night lying in Jaylen's arms and doing things, nasty things, that I'd dreamed of doing since the very first time that I'd laid eyes on him.

I knew that I should feel guilty. I just had sex with a married man. Hell, I had orchestrated the entire incident. But I couldn't. Not when my mind kept taking me back to the way he looked me in the eyes and told me repeatedly how beautiful I was. Or, the way he curled up in my bed and pulled me so close to him that it was hard to tell where his body ended and mine began.

I sat at my desk, trying to type up a memo, but could not stop thinking about the feel of his hands on my thighs and I couldn't help remembering the way that he murmured my name as he made love to me.

At one point, Mitra kidded with me that I should have probably taken the day off. She'd walked behind me and tapped me on the shoulder and I practically jumped to the ceiling.

"Omigod, Tracey. You're as fidgety and jumpy as a whore on Communion Sunday. Are you hung over or something? Did you hook up with Chef Cutie after we left? Come on, give it up! What's going on with you?" She shot questions at me so rapid fast that it made my head hurt trying to keep up with her barrage and try to figure out what I was going to tell her to change the subject.

"Yeah," I nervously chuckled. "You've found out my secret. After you guys left last night I doubled back to the restaurant and kidnapped Chef Cutie. I tied him up with my Second Line bandana and made him my sex slave. He's still shackled to my bed post as we speak.

No, seriously, though. I am horrible at holding my liquor. My head is pounding, I'm seriously hung over."

"Aw, poor thing," she said, backing down and practically pushing me into her black leather swivel chair. "Here, sit down and I'll make you some tea."

I sat in the chair and rolled my eyes up to the ceiling. Now I was really batting a thousand. In just a few hours I'd turned into a liar as well as a cheat.

I don't know what made me feel worse. The fact that Mitra spent the entire morning trying to help me recoup from a hangover that I didn't even have, or the fact that Jaylen hadn't showed his face in the office yet, even though I checked and knew that he didn't have any appointments that should have kept him out of the office. I was beginning to wonder if he was purposely keeping away from me. If he'd woke up regretting the time that we'd spent together and was sitting at home trying to find a way to untangle me from his life.

By mid-afternoon I was approaching full panic mode. After running countless scenarios through my mind of Jaylen calling me into his office and letting me down easy, I couldn't take it anymore so I made my excuses to Mitra and Byron, gathered my belongings and got ready to get out of there.

I was walking out of the door when Jaylen was walking in. We practically bumped straight into one another.

"Hi," I muttered, or something like that.

"Hi," he replied. "How are you doing?"

Oddly, he did not stop to hear my answer. I stood there, unsure if I should stay or walk away, but before I was able to decide he turned around and whispered, "Six o'clock, tonight?"

I nodded my head yes and turned to walk out of the door.

Verse thirty: all the man I need

By the time 6:00 arrived I had changed outfits three times and cleaned the apartment from top to bottom before deciding to strategically throw a few items here and there so it wouldn't look like I was trying so hard.

I answered his knock at my door wearing a big smile and nothing else. Just kidding! I was wearing gray sweats and a white tank top. Again, I didn't want to appear as if I was trying too hard. I couldn't remember a time when I'd felt more nervous. I kept fidgeting with the locks before I was finally able to disengage them, and when I eventually got the door open, I was unsure of what to do with my hands.

I looked into his eyes and wanted to jump into his arms, right where we left off last night, but I wasn't sure if he was feeling the same way. Maybe he was here, standing before me to tell me that it was over. I stepped back to let him in.

The first thing he said surprised me.

"I can't believe how nervous I am."

"Ha," I laughed. "You're nervous? My hands are shaking." I said, holding them up so he could see the tremor.

He smiled and took both of my hands into his.

"Do you regret it?" he asked.

Before he could barely finish his question, I shook my head emphatically and told him, "No, I don't. What about you?"

"No, I don't" he echoed. "I know I probably should, but I don't. I spent the whole morning waiting for the guilt to come, but it's just not there. I do not feel guilty. I keep reminding myself *why* I should feel guilty, but every time I come up with a good one, your beautiful face appears in my head" He smiled and then added, "Or my mind takes me back to the way that it felt being with you last night...to the cute little noises that you make when you like what's happening to you."

I took my hands away from his and used them to cover my face. "Oh my gosh, I don't make noises," I proclaimed.

"You do, and it's adorable. Everything about you is adorable."

I was sitting back, basking in his words when I suddenly sat up, worried. "Wait a minute, this thing, between us...is this only about sex?"

"No, no, of course not," he assured me. "I'm sorry if I made it seem that way. Tracey, I don't think you understand how crazy I am about you. How happy it makes me, just thinking about being with you. I'm not trying to sound conceited, but I could have sex with just about anyone.

No, that doesn't sound right either, does it?" he asked, looking like he was trying to find a way to get his foot out of his mouth. "I'm just saying that there have been a few occasions where I could have strayed outside of my marriage. But I didn't. To be honest with you, even though my wife and I didn't get married under the most ideal conditions, I never really felt the desire to. I'm not going to say that I do not love my wife, or that I am no longer attracted to her, because that would not be entirely true. I don't know what I am doing here. The only thing that I *do* know is that from the moment you sat in that chair in my office I knew that everything had changed.

"So, what happens if I fall in love with you?" I asked, taking his hand back in mine.

He thought about my question for a moment before answering, "I'll try not to let you down."

I thought about his wife, probably sitting at home waiting for him to get home, and I whispered, more to myself than to him, "How can you not?"

Verse thirty-one: creepin'

The light from the votive candles cast a shadow across Jaylen's face, causing him to look even more mysterious than he already was to me. I don't think that he set out to be this man of mystery, It's just that that there was so much that I wanted to know about him that no matter how much he shares with me I feel that it is never enough.

We were nested in a secluded section of the Hotel Indigo in downtown Baton Rouge, roughly an hour outside of New Orleans, and I was as excited as a little kid on Christmas morning. Jaylen and I had been "dating" for over three months and this was the first time that I was able to have him all to myself for a whole day, and a whole night.

The room was empty except for a piano player who was playing smooth jazz that had me swaying in my seat and an interracial couple sitting a few tables over. The way they couldn't seem to keep their hands off one another made me wonder if they were stealing time. Just like us.

It was obvious that Jaylen was anxious to head upstairs and get me in bed, but he was humoring me, allowing me the fantasy of pretending what we were a real couple, at least for a little while.

"So, Ms. Dubois," he said, tilting his Apple Martini my way. "What did you do all day while I was at my meeting?'

I pictured myself running around all afternoon like a maniac trying to find the perfect outfit for our special night. Something classy, yet at the same time something sexy enough that he would want to tear it off me.

"Not much," I answered coyly. "I browsed around the outlet mall that we passed on our way out here and then I relaxed in the hot tub, daydreaming about spending the night with you."

A top-heavy waitress came over and asked if we needed anything else. Jaylen ordered a Rum and Coke and I traded in my Strawberry Daiquiri for something a little sexier—Sex on the Beach.

"Be right back," the waitress said and then waddled away. I was amazed that she was able to stay upright with those triple Ds. To his credit, Jaylen didn't stare at them, too much.

Once Dolly Parton Jr. was gone, I asked the question that I'd been wondering about all day.

"How is it you're able to spend the night with me? Where does she think you are?"

I held my breath and waited for the answer. Though he was usually straight forward with his answers to me, I could tell that Jaylen did not like it when I brought up his wife or his marriage.

He took a sip of his drink, probably trying to keep his patience with me, and then said, "Actually, she didn't ask."

I raised my eyebrow at him. "She didn't ask?"

"No, she didn't. She hardly asks, or tells me anything anymore."

I sat up taller in my seat. Jaylen hardly ever talks about his wife. He's certainly never indicated that things may be less than ideal at home. Though of course I always assumed it, since he's fooling around with me.

Jaylen didn't need nudging to continue, the alcohol must have loosened his tongue. He took another sip and said, "Half of the time she acts like she likes it better when I'm not there."

I looked at him as if he was talking gibberish. Here I was doing everything in my power to scrape together every minute I could get with this man, and he was telling me that his own wife doesn't like having him around? What was she, crazy?

I thought about mama's advice, 'don't ask questions that you are unprepared for the answer to', but I had to ask anyway. I needed to know.

"Jaylen, tell me about her. About the two of you."

"What do you want to know?"

"Whatever you want to tell," I answered.

He shrugged and said, "There's not much to tell. Our mothers were best friends so I guess it was almost expected that we would end up together. We were high school sweethearts and then we went off to college. She went to Spelman and I went to Morehouse. We were still going out, but once we got away from our parents, we started seeing other people as well. Anyway, long story short, Linda wound up getting pregnant our senior year. Of course, I did the right thing and married her, but she lost the baby a few months later."

My arm broke out in goosebumps when Jaylen mentioned losing his baby. As Ma-Me would say, 'felt like someone just walked across my grave.'

"Aw, Jaylen, I'm sorry," I said. I placed my hand over his and let it rest there.

"Thanks, but it was a long time ago," he said.

"So, what's going on now? Do you regret marrying her?" I asked and held my breath, waiting for his answer.

As usual, he was totally honest with me. "No, I don't regret marrying her. We probably wouldn't have gotten married so soon, but it was bound to happen anyway. What I regret was the way that I handled things after she lost the baby. I should have made sure that she got some type of counseling or something. It was obvious that she was having a hard time, but so was I. We were young and didn't know how to be there for one another. Communication pretty much stopped altogether."

I could see the sadness in his eyes. It made my heart hurt for him. For both of them.

Jaylen could sense the change in my mood so he attempted to lighten things up.

"Anyway, enough of this depressing talk," he said, grabbing my hand and lifting me out of my seat. "We're on our first date, remember, so let's go and get this party started!"

Verse thirty-two: sorry doesn't always make it right

I had barely gotten the *hello* out of my mouth before mama started in on me. As if I didn't feel bad enough as it was. I still couldn't believe that I'd missed Jazzmine's church solo. Granted, my appearances at Mount Zion Baptist Church were few and far in between ever since JP and the messed-up way that they treated me after I got pregnant with Jazzmine. But I didn't have an excuse in the world for missing my daughter's big performance. I had been so wrapped up in my romance with Jaylen that it simply slipped my mind.

Ok, it hadn't really slipped my mind. I woke up with every intention of attending church services and listening to my little angel sing, but when Jaylen called and informed me that his wife was summoned into the office and he had the morning free I simply couldn't resist the desire to be with him. I honestly thought that I would have time to meet Jaylen for a quick breakfast and still make it in time for Jazz's solo. But our quick breakfast turned into a not so quick make out session which evolved into a love making session that lasted most of the afternoon, and before I knew it I was walking into church at the exact moment that Reverend Howard was giving the final benediction.

I slipped in the pew next to mama and she didn't skip a beat before turning to me and hissing, "I can't believe you. You knew how important this was to Jazzy."

"I'm sorry, ma," I began. "I got tied up..." and then Ma-Me twisted around in her seat and gave us a look that shut us both up.

"I'll deal with you at the house," she spat at me.

Ma-Me planned the Sunday brunch of all Sunday brunches in celebration of Jazzmine's first church solo. Not only were the Dubois in the house, but she had also invited Reverend Howard, Mrs. Boudreaux, Mrs. Collins, the youth choir director, and a few of Jazzmine's friends from church.

I threw myself into hostess mode and tried my best to make the celebration everything that Jazzmine could possibly want, but still, I found myself on the receiving end of awkward silences and dirty glances everywhere I turned. Even sweet Lynette, who made a point of never taking sides in any argument or disagreement, managed to shoot me a disparaged look or two.

Jazzmine was running around the house looking like a princess in a pink lace dress and her hair in long ponytails with bouncy, Shirley Temple-like curls. She seemed to be innocuously playing tag with her friends, but I could tell by the way that she avoided eye contact with me that she was disappointed in me also. I felt like shit.

I was sitting at the kitchen table, picking blueberries out of a slice of coffee cake, trying to figure out how I was going to make it up to her, when Greg and his mother walked through the door.

Greg started towards me with a huge grin on his face and before I knew it, I was wrapped in his arms in another of his smothering bear hugs. I must admit, it did feel kind of nice to have someone in the house that did not seem to think that I was up for the suckiest mother of the year award.

"Trace with the face! How you doing, lady?" Greg asked, picking me up and lifting me off my feet.

"Trace with the face?" I laughed, remembering back to the days when he was the nerdiest kid on the block. "Really, Greg?"

He beamed down at me, looking all grown and sexy, yet little boy cute at the same time in faded Levi jeans and a light blue Polo shirt.

"Girl, look at you," he grinned. "Still as beautiful as ever."

I made my way back to my chair, feeling surprisingly shy and a bit overwhelmed with all the day's occurrences. Memories of my morning with Jaylen flashed through my mind, causing a quick flurry of butterflies in my stomach, but they were quickly replaced with feelings of regret and guilt for having missed my daughter's big moment. I couldn't remember a time where I had ever felt such conflicting emotions.

Greg lowered himself into the chair next to mine, popped a few of my discarded blueberries into his mouth and began filling me in on the last five years of his life.

Long story short; culinary school at the Art Institute of New York, an internship with a mentor that took him under his wing and taught him all his secrets, an unexpected inheritance from a father that he barely knew, and finally, moving back to New Orleans six months ago and opening The G Spot. All exciting and impressive sounding stuff, which made me feel uneasy and even a tad bit defensive when he finished his inspiring tale and I knew that it was my turn to share.

For some reason I felt that my account of being a single mother, part-time lounge singer, and full-time mistress to my married boss, would not come across as quite as impressive.

For once, I was grateful for the distraction when Ma-Me came barreling into the kitchen, complaining that the kids were making too much noise and spilling soft drinks on the carpet. She was ready to shut the party down so Greg took the hint, said his goodbyes and promised to keep in touch.

I smiled as I closed the door behind him. I could tell by the way he held me just a beat too long that he was not totally over his childhood crush on me.

I was placing the last few dishes in the dishwasher when Lynette came into the kitchen, picked up a dish towel and began wiping down the countertop.

I held my breath and waited for her to ask the question that I was sure she'd wanted to ask all day.

She finished the countertop and started scrubbing the stovetop before turning to me and asking, "Tracey, where were you today? Why did you miss Jazzmine's solo?"

I knew this moment was coming, but still I hadn't decided if I would tell her the truth or not. I felt the exact same way that I felt when I found out that I was pregnant. That I was about to disclose something to my sister that would change the way she looked at me forever. I closed the dishwasher, slowly took a seat at the breakfast bar, and contritely told Lynette everything.

"I know that I shouldn't, but I love him," is how I ended my spiel.

"How can you love him?" Lynette asked. "You don't even know him."

"Of course, I know him," I argued. "We spend every day together. I know everything about that man. Probably more than his wife even knows."

Lynette shook her head and disputed me. "But that's the thing, Trace, you are not his wife. And though you beg to differ, I stand by what I just said. You really *don't* know him. You only know the tiny bit that he allows you to see when you are with him. You think its love, but relationships like these are illusions. They're not real. It's only part-time so you only get the best of one another. You don't get the day to day, sometimes boring aspects of a true relationship."

I stared at her as if she was speaking in Pig Latin. How dare she sit there and try to tell me that what Jaylen and I have is not real.

"I know that I'm not telling you what you want to hear," she said, as if able to read my mind, "but hey, that's what family is all about, right? Loving you enough to tell you that something is shit, even when you're trying to pass it off as steak."

Verse thirty-three: a house is not a home

The next afternoon, with Lynette's words still floating around in my mind, I made my way into the gated English Turn subdivision. I pulled in front of Jaylen's house and just sat there staring at it. It was a two-story stucco mini-mansion with massive white columns and a Spanish-style roof. Exactly what I pictured him living in.

I found the spare key under the planter where Jaylen said I would, and walked through the front door as if I had every right in the world to be there. But as soon as I entered the foyer and closed the door behind me, I was assaulted with a sense of unease and guilt so strong that it nearly brought me to my knees. I knew that I had no right to be inside this woman's house.

In my defense, coming here was not my idea. Jaylen called, practically begging me to stop by his house to pick up a file that he'd left on his desk; and saying no him didn't seem to be an option for me, so I grabbed my keys and made my way across town, directly to a location that I'd promised myself that I would never visit.

It was not my intention to snoop, I swear, it wasn't. I planned on grabbing the file and getting out of there as soon as possible, but as I walked through Jaylen's home, the place he went when he was away from me, I couldn't help taking in my surroundings. I couldn't help wondering what he was like when he was here. With her.

Entering the spacious den, I did a double take at the soaring ceilings, double crown moldings and spiral staircase. I knew that Jaylen and his wife were doing well, but damn!

The room was painted a warm beige color and was decorated with cream linen furniture that looked so expensive and immaculate that I was nervous even walking past it, never mind attempting to sit down and get comfortable in it. I couldn't help but wonder what passed through Jaylen's mind on the dozens of occasions that we'd made out on my second-hand puke colored Ikea sectional.

I kept it moving, peeking in on the kitchen—stainless steel and granite all over the place, of course, and then made my way up the stairs to Jaylen's office. I proceeded down the hall to the second door on the left, which Jaylen informed me was his home office and was about to turn the doorknob to enter and retrieve the files that I was looking for, when I glanced to my right and realized that their bedroom door was open.

I couldn't help myself. I walked towards the room as if I was in a trance, and before I knew it I was standing in front of their king-sized bed, looking down at the place that he laid his head at night.

The room smelled of him. Sandalwood and coconut oil. I closed my eyes and breathed in deeply, suddenly missing him fiercely. Suddenly, I wanted nothing more than to get back to the office. Back to him.

I was about to turn around and walk out of the door when I noticed their wedding picture on the bedside table. I walked over and picked it up, surprised by the heaviness of the crystal frame. I studied the picture as if I was being quizzed on it later. Jaylen was standing behind his beaming bride, holding her tightly. Their smiling faces seemed to challenge anyone who ever doubted true love.

I put the frame down and walked out of their house.

Verse thirty-four: is it a crime

"Goddamn it to hell!" Mitra shrieked, slamming the phone back into its cradle and upsetting the mound of phone messages that were stacked next to it.

Hearing Mitra curse around the office was no big jaw dropper for me, albeit that outburst was a tad louder than I've ever heard from her before. But what caused my mouth to fly open and made me wonder what in the world was going on was the crazed, yet anguished look, on her face. She looked as if she'd been sucker punched. Or at the very least, looking for some sucker to punch.

I did not intend for that sucker to be me.

My first instinct was to do an about face and stealthily make my way back into the ladies room and pretend that I had not been a witness to her tirade, but compassion got the best of me, so I took a deep breath and decided to go and see if there was any way that I could help her out. I figured that the least I could do was relieve her at the reception desk for a moment so she could go to the break room and pull herself together.

"Mitra, sweetie, what's the matter?" I asked, approaching her slowly and apprehensively, as if she was some exotic uncaged animal.

"Arggghh! I am so mad I could fucking spit!" she yelled, causing me to raise my hands in peace at her and take two large steps backwards.

This coaxed a slight smile from her so I decided that comedy might do the trick.

"Tell me who the dude is," I teased. "We'll bust the windows out of his car."

"The dude is my papa," she responded, shocking me, "and we'd have to fly over 17 hours to bust the windows out of that fucker's car."

Being a part of such a tight knit, though admittedly slightly dysfunctional, family, it disturbed me to hear Mitra speak so callously about her father. I couldn't imagine anything that my mom, or even Ma-Me, could do to make to react so disrespectfully towards them. I decided to keep my mouth closed and wait to see what Mitra would decide to share with me about her family's issues.

"I just can't believe that he would betray my mother that way," she continued.

"What did he do?" I asked, figuring that it couldn't be a worse indiscretion than most of the other dead-beat dads that I knew, including my own.

"He just told my mother that he is taking another wife," she replied, shocking me for the second time in under five minutes.

"Wow," I responded, plopping down into the seat that she had previously vacated. "That's deep. Can he do that? Is that an acceptable part of y'all culture?"

She sat down in a chair opposite mine and considered my questions before answering, "Legally, yes, he can. And morally, he can. According to the Quran, the holy book of Islam, a man can have up to four wives at a time. Having that many wives is very rare, but it is not unusual for an Emirate man to have two wives at the same time if they are able to afford to care for them. But the thing is, my mother is not an Emirate. She is from Eastern Europe, and he promised her when they married that he would not take any other wives."

"Dang, that's messed up," I replied, trying to put myself in Mitra's mother's position. "How is she taking this?"

"She's friggin' furious," Mitra answered, rising from the chair she was sitting in and returning to pacing up and down the office. "She doesn't deserve this. She has been the perfect wife to him for twenty-five years and now all a sudden he is pulling this shit on her."

"No disrespect to your mom, Mitra, but if she has been such a perfect wife, why do you think your dad feels the need to have someone else in his life?"

I couldn't help but compare Mitra's parent's predicament with my relationship to Jaylen. I couldn't count the number of nights that I stayed up wondering how Jaylen could claim to be in love with both me and his wife at the same time.

Now, I couldn't help wondering if he would choose to take me as his second wife if it was morally acceptable in our society and he was given the opportunity. Would I even go for something so preposterous? It was disturbing to me, but I honestly could not answer that question at that moment.

I had traveled so far into my own mind that it took me a moment to realize that Mitra was attempting to answer my question.

"Papa would not come to the phone and speak to me; he said that it was none of my concern, but mother, in between her sobbing, said that he simply fell in love with someone else.

"How could he do that?" She continued. "After all this time, how can he possibly think that he loves someone else?"

"I don't know, Mitra," I began cautiously, suddenly feeling very defensive and supportive of both her dad and this other woman. "People change... their wants and their needs... maybe this woman makes him happy."

"Pshhh," She spat. "Wants and needs my behind! And I don't even want to talk about her home wrecking ass! Besides, it is not her place to make him happy. He already has a wife to keep him happy. She needs to find a man of her own to make happy!"

"That's the problem with people today," She continued on, barely taking a breath. "They think that they can do whatever they want and simply blame it on love."

"Yeah, but you have to admit, sometimes the heart makes you do things that you would never think that you'd do," I countered, probably more in my own defense then in defense of her father.

"That's bull, Tracey," Mitra contradicted. "I'm not saying that I don't believe in love. It's the falling in and out part that I have a problem with. When someone says that they have fallen in love that statement is telling me that they are choosing to do something. And when you have already committed yourself to someone then you need to *choose* to remain faithful and monogamous to that person. When you are single and you think that you are attracted to someone that is already married, you need to *choose* to respect the vows that were taken between two people before God. Simple, point blank."

I didn't have any words to argue against Mitra, so I simply gave her a hug and told her that I would be praying for her parents, and made a mental note to pray for myself as well.

Verse thirty-five: secret lovers

The next morning Jaylen and I met at The Trolley Stop; a quaint little streetcar turned restaurant, for breakfast and a little under the table hand holding, before reporting to the office. We didn't normally take our little show on the road, but I was getting tired of hiding all the time. I promised Jaylen that I would behave and pretend that we were having a business meeting if anyone happened to see us together, and he reluctantly agreed.

"You look beautiful, as always," Jaylen said as he slid into the chair across from me. You know I started blushing.

"You look great as well," I said, and beamed over at him. Jaylen was wearing a navy-blue business suit with a crisp white shirt and a red power tie. He looked like he could have been Barack's younger brother.

"So, were you able to get Jazzmine off to school on time this morning?" he asked as he looked over the menu.

I laughed as I recalled the adventure that I've been having trying to get Jazzmine ready for preschool. Only four years old and already she was such a drama queen. She had to wear the perfect outfit with perfectly coordinated accessories. Yesterday I made the mistake of trying to dress her in a pair of blue jeans and Jazz had a fit. Told me that blue jeans were for the playground, school was a place for dresses. What can I say? You just have to love that little girl.

Jaylen was always asking me about Jazzmine and hinting around about meeting her but I wasn't sure that was a great idea. I am very protective about the people that I introduce my daughter to, especially those that I happen to be dating. I didn't want to confuse her by parading a string of "uncles" in front of her that she may not ever see again after a few weeks.

"Yes," I answered with a smile. "She was dressed as a perfect little princess this morning."

I then decided to steer the conversation to something that had been pressing on my mind. "Have you heard from Mitra this morning? Is she up to coming into the office?" I asked as I blew into my cup of coffee.

Jaylene had gotten an earful from Mitra so he was aware of her parent's marital situation, but he was disappointedly mum on the matter. I tried to nudge the conversation towards that direction, without being totally obvious, by saying inconspicuous things like,

'*Mitra's dad is a trip, huh*' and '*I hope Mitra's parents are able to work things out.*'

I wanted to know where his head was on the subject; especially as it related to being in love with two people at the same time, but coming right out and asking about his views on the subject seemed a little, I don't know, needy or something.

"Jaylen, are you paying attention to me?" I asked after he'd failed to respond.

"I'm sorry," he said, looking up from his cell phone. "No, I haven't spoken to Mitra, but I'm sure that she'll be in."

Jaylen seemed uncharacteristically preoccupied at the restaurant; checking his phone often, though I'd never heard it ring, and glancing towards the front door when he thought that I was studying the menu. I wanted to ask him what was on his mind, but I was afraid to.

Mama always warned us about asking question that we were unprepared for the answers to. I thought about this advice often as I was dealing with Jaylen. I tried not to inquire about his marriage, or even harp too much over where this relationship was headed. I was always afraid of what his answer would be. So instead of picking his brain about the uncertainties of our relationship I made a mental list of the things that I *was* sure of.

I was sure that he had genuine feelings for me. Not only was he great at verbalizing his feelings, but he also demonstrated then to me on a daily basis, with little things like random emails complimenting an outfit or a hairstyle, a slight squeeze of my hand when no one was looking, or flowers delivered from a so-called "secret admirer." He also loved to spoil me with materials things. I glanced down at the Tiffany bracelet that he'd given me for Valentine's Day and I couldn't help but smile as I remembered the way I'd shown my appreciation for such an expensive and thoughtful gift.

It was obvious that he enjoyed spending time with me. I know that it sounds cliché, but I honestly felt that we were friends as well as lovers. We laughed at the same things, shared the same tastes in food and music, and could talk for hours, oftentimes about the most mundane of topics.

But I also knew that he was conflicted by me. As the Facebook status goes: *it's complicated*. And no matter how much pleasure we found in one another, both in and out of bed, once we left our cocoon and were forced back into the real world, we both knew that boundaries had to be respected and a degree of decorum had to be followed.

By the time I made it back to Baker and Brewer there was a mountain of work waiting for me. Mitra decided to take a personal day after all to deal with her family's issues, so I was manning the front desk in addition to tackling Mitra's typing and correspondence duties.

It was after two before I realized that I had worked straight through lunch. I felt my stomach grumble in protest and was trying to decide how I was going to appease it when the phone rang.

"Baker and Brewer," I answered.

"Hello gorgeous," Jaylen murmured. "What are you doing up there? I miss you."

"Not much," I blushed into the phone. "Just trying to figure out what I want for lunch."

"I'm hungry too," he replied. "But I already know what I feel like eating."

And just like that, with so few words, I feel my body react. Goodness gracious, the things this man could do to me. I quickly racked my brain trying to think of an equally sexy reply when I heard someone walk into the reception area.

"Hold on, sweetie," I purred. "Someone just walked into the office."

"Good afternoon. Welcome to Baker and Brewer," I said, taking a quick peek at the appointment book to see if I had overlooked a booking. "How may I help you?"

"I'm here to see my husband," she replied. "Mr. Jaylen Baker."

It felt like a million minutes passed before I was finally able to make my mouth move, and even longer before my brain was able to catch up.

I was looking straight into the eyes of the other woman!

Verse thirty-six: the other woman

I guess it seems weird for me to refer to Jaylen's wife as *the other woman*, but that is what she seemed like to me. I know that it was foolish and naïve of me, selfish even, but I considered Jaylen mine, and having her walk into "our" office felt like a violation. As if she was invading my space. Just like that, I went from being stunned to being pissed!

And then my thoughts switched to Jaylen. I wondered how he would handle this situation; his wife and his lover in the same place at the same time. Would this be the circumstance that finally caused Mr. Cool to break out in a sweat? Seemed like I was about to find out.

I picked up the phone to inform Mr. Baker that Mrs. Baker was in the office to see him and then I replaced the phone into its receiver, seemingly in slow motion, and then I let my eyes travel the length of Mrs. Linda Baker.

I knew that I wouldn't have much time to scrutinize her. I figured that Jaylen would be tripping over his feet to get to the reception area to put some distance between us; and I was right. A good sixty seconds barely passed before Jaylen was standing in front of us, ushering his wife into his office. I couldn't take my eyes off his hands at the small her back as he led her away, a place that his hands had been on me just a few short hours before.

It took a while for me to realize that I was still standing there, staring at his closed office door, before I came to my senses and returned to my seat behind my desk.

I felt numb, but the same thought kept running through my mind. *So, this is the person that Jaylen decided to marry. This is the person that Jaylen has pledged his heart and his life to.*

She was pretty. I couldn't deny that. But then again, I didn't expect otherwise. Jaylen liked to surround himself with attractive and expensive looking things.

I couldn't help but compare her to myself. She was taller than me, probably around 5'8 or 5'9. But then again, I had to take into consideration the fact that she was wearing at least four-inch Jimmy Choo's.

I wouldn't say that she was prettier than me, but she was definitely more polished looking. I glanced down at the black slacks and gray blouse that I had painstakingly picked out at the Gap the week before and felt embarrassed that I considered this my "good" work outfit. I was sure that that jade green pantsuit that she wore cost more than my entire month's salary.

I noticed that she had gained weight since their wedding day photo. She wasn't fat, not quite, but then again, she wasn't more than a Twinkie or two away from shocking the scale. I wondered what Jaylen thought about that, considering that he was always complementing my petite frame.

I found myself wondering what it was about her that ultimately attracted Jaylen to her. I knew that she was smart. Jaylen once mentioned that she graduated at the top of her class and I knew that she was a civil defense lawyer, so I knew that she was contributing her share financially. But what else? Was she funnier than me, kinder than me? Easier to get along with than me? I wanted so badly to know what made him pick her. And most importantly, I wanted to know, if he had the chance to do it all again, who would he pick: her or me?

I couldn't put myself through the torment of watching them walk out together, so I shut down my computer, gathered my belongings, and sulked out the door.

Once I made it back to my apartment, I found that I had a restless energy that I couldn't dispel. Jaylen and I had plans to grab an early dinner together, but after not hearing from him for a couple of hours I figured those plans were squashed. I began throwing a few items in a bowl to make a tossed salad when my phone rang. I tried to act blasé, but I couldn't even fool myself. I lunged at it. I couldn't wait to hear what Jaylen had to say.

Verse thirty-seven: dancing in the street

The crisp sounds of the trumpets and the resonance of the drums had my feet tapping and my hips doing an involuntary little wiggle. I had to admit, I was enjoying my afternoon out with Greg, even though my first inclination was to give him a resounding no when he called and asked me to go out with him.

I was so surprised that it was Greg, and not Jaylen, calling me that it took me a moment to get my bearings and actually make sense of what he was asking me.

"Come on, Trace," he pressured when he heard the hesitation in my voice. "I'm not asking for your hand in marriage. I'm just inviting an old friend to keep me company for a little while. You can even bring

Jazzmine if you're scared to be alone with me," he teased. "The French Quarter Festival is this weekend and the weather is perfect. She'll enjoy running around Jackson Square, and who knows, you might even mess around and have a good time."

I tried, I really did, but I could not think of a single reason to refuse his request. My heart was trying to persuade me to stay home and wait to hear from Jaylen, but my head was telling me that he had chosen the person what he wanted to be with, and apparently that person wasn't me. Nonetheless, my heart, as usual, was winning the debate.

I opened my mouth to tell Greg no, but my words came out sounding a lot like yes, and before I even knew what was happening, Jazz and I were hanging out in the French Quarters with Mr. Gregory Adams.

Greg was right. Jazzmine was having the time of her life at the festival and so was her mother. Being with Greg felt easy and light; reminded me of afternoons jumping Double Dutch, slurping frozen cups, and trash talking on mama's front porch.

The Quarters were packed with people; young and old, black and white, straight and gay. It was a regular melting pot out there. Intoxicating smells of delicious food were intermingled with the sweaty and pissy smell of the French Quarter streets, but that simply added to the ambiance.

"This is nice, isn't it?" Greg asked.

"Yes, it is," I agreed.

"I'm thinking about having the G Spot participate in the festival next year. Set up under one of those tents over there. What do you think?"

"I think that's a great idea. You should definitely do it," I enthusiastically replied.

"So, if I set up shop out here next year will you come out and work with me?" he asked.

"I'll think about it. Who knows, you may not even want to be in my company a year from now," I replied.

"Yeah, I'm sure that you are going to work on my nerves so much before this day is over that I will never speak to you again," he joked.

"Come on, Tracey," Greg said, suddenly turning very serious. Now that I have you back in my life after all this time, do you think I am going to let you get away so easily?

I wasn't sure how to answer that question so I turned to Jazzmine and pretended that she needed my immediate attention.

Jazzmine was a bundle of energy and could barely reign in her enthusiasm. She was hopping up and down on one foot, itching to find something to get into.

"Calm down, Itty Bitty," Greg smiled at her and tugged on one of her long ponytails, which was slightly higher than the other, thanks to Ma-Me and her horrible hair combing skills. "We're gonna have some fun, I promise."

I couldn't help but smile back at him. I loved how natural he was with Jazzmine. It also made me feel wistful. Made me wonder just how short I was selling myself and my daughter for falling in love with Jaylen, someone who would never truly be mine; instead of someone that I could possibly build a life and have a future with. Someone like Greg.

We made it home long past Jazz's bedtime. I carried her up the stairs and tucked her into bed and then I went through the motions of unwinding. Though I was as tired as a Hebrew Slave I was having a hard time shutting down my mind.

After soaking in a warm bath, I turned my radio to Sunday Night Slow Jams, lit lavender scented incense and let my mind ruminate over the events of the past few days. Jaylen's wife coming to the office was a definite eye opener to me. For the first time I was forced to pair a face with the name. An actual human being to the obscure figure that I tried so hard to pretend didn't even exist.

And then there's Greg. He has become such a dear friend to me, but I know that our feelings towards one another are not on the same level. The last thing that I want to do is to hurt him.

All these thoughts were spinning through my mind as Luther Vandross tried his best to serenade me to sleep.

Verse thirty-eight: delicious

Jaylen hadn't called me the entire weekend and Monday morning he had the nerve to try to and act as if everything was honky-dory. I gave him the side-eye when he told me good morning, and walked to the break room to put on a pot of coffee without speaking to him. He followed behind me and wrapped his arms around my waist, a careless move that he'd never attempted at the office before. I could feel my knees getting weak and my resolve floundering, but I willed myself to stay strong. He hurt me and he should know it. I side-stepped out of his embrace.

He grabbed my hand and turned me around to face him. "Baby, I'm sorry. I know that you're upset with me."

I didn't say anything, so he continued talking. "I wanted to see you, or at the very least, call you, but I never had a moment to myself."

"The whole weekend," I hissed, feeling tears threatening to fall. "You're telling me that over a two-day period you couldn't squeeze out five minutes to let me know that everything was alright?"

"I swear," he proclaimed. "It's like she tried to glue herself to me this weekend. I don't know what was going on with her."

I didn't respond, so he went on "Even when we were at Trolley Stop, I kept thinking that she was going to call me or walk through the door."

So, that's why he was acting so nervous and paranoid, I thought.

"Do you think she knows about us," I worriedly asked, forgetting for a moment that I was mad at him.

I wasn't sure how I felt about that possibility. I'd always tried my best to be as inconspicuous and careful as possible. Jaylen and I made a point to avoid any physical contact around the office and we kept our communication with each other to a minimum. I rarely ever called him first; never sure if she was around. Instead, I waited for him to reach out to me. As much as I wanted Jaylen all to myself, I knew that having his wife find out about us would hurt him deeply and I loved him far too much to be the intentional cause of that.

And, just to keep it real, I was also seriously concerned with what would become of our relationship once his wife found out about us. I knew that it would change things, but the question was: would it be for the better or for the worst? Would she leave him, giving Jaylen and me an opportunity to embark upon a *real* relationship together? Or would she give him an ultimatum, forcing him to leave me?

"I don't think that she knows about us," he answered. "I can't imagine her knowing and not confronting me about it. It's not normally her style to holds things in like that. But she has been playing me so close lately. I can't help wondering if she is beginning to get a little suspicious."

I bit my lower lip, wondering how to proceed with the conversation. "So, what now?" I asked, dreading his answer to my question.

"Nothing new," he responded. "We keep going the way we have been going. Of course, we'll continue to be careful, but other than that..." he trailed off.

I let out a whiff of breath that I wasn't even aware that I had been holding. I threw myself into his arms and kissed him passionately, forgetting just that fast what he'd said about us being more careful.

"It's okay, I understand. I didn't have anything special planned," I lied, turning the burner off from under the pot of gumbo that I had spent all day making for Jaylen. "I'll just see you tomorrow."

"I'm so sorry, baby," he apologized. "She told me about this thing at the last minute. I can't think of a way to get out of it."

"Don't worry about it," I said, hoping to get off the phone before my true emotions came out. "Just call me in the morning."

"I will. Goodnight, my baby."

"Yeah, goodnight," I returned, before hanging up the phone and sinking down into the sofa.

Later that night when Greg called, I wasn't surprised or disappointed. I was happy to have a distraction from thinking about Jaylen, wondering where our relationship was headed.

"Hey, what are you getting into tonight?" he asked, sounding his usual, laid back self.

"I don't know," I answered. "I was thinking about picking Jazzmine up and taking her to the movies, but I could probably be talked into something else," I joked. "What do you have in mind?"

"I was about to swing by the restaurant and I thought you might have fun tagging along."

"You want me to come and watch you work?" I laughed. "That does not exactly sound like my idea of a good time."

"Listen up, baby girl, anytime with the G Man is sure to be a good time. Now, get out of those raggedy house shoes and throw on something cute. I'll be there to pick you up in twenty minutes."

I couldn't help but chuckle at his pompousness. Where in the world did this cocky Gregory Adams come from? The pudgy little thing that I remembered from back in the days never had even an ounce of swag.

"Alright, G Man. But I'll have you know, nothing I own is raggedy," I countered, making a mental note to hide my scruffy pink slippers in the back of my closet before he got to my apartment.

We didn't make it to The G Spot until after ten. Things were winding down by then but I could tell that they'd had a pretty busy night by the harried look of the waiters rushing to and from their stations, and the thick crowd of people still surrounding the bar.

Greg's entire demeanor changed once he walked through the doors of his restaurant. He went from being the nonchalant, fun loving guy who was cracking me up in the car telling stories of his *broker than a joke* days in culinary school, to reaching The G Spot and instantly morphing into boss man. It was impressive and I must admit, hella sexy.

"Good evening, Mr. Adams. Tonight's your only night off. What are you doing here?" A petit, blonde hostess, barely out of her teens, greeted us, almost tripping over the hostess stand trying to get to Greg.

'Calm your ass down', I wanted to say to her. But then I had to remind myself that Greg was just my friend and not my man.

"Hi Sam, how's it going tonight?" Greg asked, seeming not to notice that she was practically drooling over him.

"Great! We've been pretty packed all night and Chef Charles seems to still be in a good mood, so I guess there were no mishaps in the kitchen."

"Well, that's good news," Greg replied to her and then turned to me. "I can't wait for you meet Chef. He is a trip! That dude has the worst temper that I have ever seen," he laughed.

"Really?" I chuckled. "Then why do you keep him around?"

"Wait until you try his crab cakes! Take one bite and then ask me that question again." Greg took my hand and walked me further into the restaurant.

Though I'd been inside The G Spot before, I really hadn't paid much attention to the décor and layout of the restaurant. At the time, my eyes and my mind couldn't focus on anything other than Jaylen.

Greg had done a fantastic job with the place. The walls were painted a deep merlot color and the furnishings were dark oak and contemporary.

I was about to compliment Greg on the place when we were approached by an attractive, red headed lady carrying a clipboard, dressed head to toe in all black. "Hi Gregory," she said. "Glad you made it in. Can I borrow you for a minute?"

"Hey Greta. Give me a sec." Greg looked around and flagged over a passing waiter, the same one who almost felt Byron's drunken wrath during our office celebration.

"Joe, do me a favor and show Ms. Dubois to my table. Make sure that she gets whatever she wants."

Greg then turned to me, "I'm sorry, Tracey. Greta's my manager. I promise I won't be longer than a few minutes."

"No problem," I smiled at him, before being led off by Joe.

"Order the crab cakes!" Greg called after me. "You won't be disappointed!"

Greg kept his word and joined me at the table about fifteen minutes later. By that time, I was well into my second crab cake. I'd also ordered a bowl of gumbo and grilled catfish, two dishes that I remembered loving from my last visit to the restaurant.

It didn't take more than a few bites to figure out exactly what Greg meant. Chef Charles could throw temper tantrums all day long, as long as he was turning out food like this, he was okay in my book.

Greg settled himself into the chair across from me and immediately reached across the table to get a forkful of my food. "Oh, no you don't," I teased, pulling my plate away. "Get your own."

"Wow, it's like that hunh?"

"Yeah," I responded. "When it comes to these crab cakes and food like this, it is definitely like that."

Greg laughed and then leaned back in his chair and gave me a look that left me feeling a little tingly inside. I couldn't help wondering what was going on with me. This was Greg that I was sitting across from. *Greg*, not Jaylen. So, what was I doing sitting here halfway hoping that he would reach over and kiss me?

To loosen the mood I asked, "Ok, tell me the truth. Did you bring me here tonight to try and impress me?"

"Kinda," he answered, smiling over at me. "Did it work?"

"Yeah," I admitted. "Kinda."

"Good. Because, I kinda like you. A lot."

'*Whoa, what just happened here?*'

I knew that I needed to clear things up, quickly. Greg was my friend, and such a great guy. The last thing in the world that I wanted to do was to hurt him. Again. I may have had a confusing, weak moment, wondering what it would feel like to kiss him, but Jaylen was my baby. The only person that I wanted to end my night with. *Right?*

"Greg," I began, "I'm sorry if I gave you the wrong impression. I'm flattered, but I'm actually seeing someone right now."

He hesitated for a moment before responding.

"I figured that. I knew that there was a very slim chance that you would be single. I just wanted to put all my cards on the table and let you know how I feel. How I've always felt."

"Oh," was all I said, because I couldn't think of anything else.

165

"So, who is this lucky guy?" Greg asked.

"Really?" I groaned and then grinned over at him. "Are we really having this conversation?"

"Yeah, why not. You brought up Mr. Wonderful. I'm just trying to find out what kind of man it takes to capture the heart of Ms. Tracey Dubois."

"Stop teasing me! And I never called him Mr. Wonderful, those are your words."

"Well, let me hear your words," he countered. "Tell me about him."

"Okaaay..." I conceded, since it was apparent that I wasn't getting let off the hook anytime soon.

"His name is Jaylen. He's a Scorpio and he enjoys long walks and picnics in the moonlight," I joked.

"I can see that singing is not your only talent. Maybe I should put you and your standup routine on the schedule on our next amateur's night," Greg said, throwing a dinner roll at me.

"It's okay, though. If you don't feel comfortable talking to me about him then I'll drop the subject."

I wasn't sure if Greg was intentionally tricking me with his little reverse psychology ploy, but whatever he was doing it was working. Suddenly, I felt defensive about my relationship. I also felt an undeniable urge to finally tell him all about Jaylen. Get a male perspective that was hopefully the opposite of Lynette's dismal take on the matter.

Verse thirty-nine: inside my love

"Wow," was what Greg said when I'd finished spilling the beans about Jaylen. "You sure don't make things easy for yourself, do you? Let's see...you're dating an older man, who also happens to be your boss, and what am I leaving out...oh yeah, let's not forget the fact that he's also married! Dang Trace, what are you doing?"

Greg's words kept repeating over and over in my mind, like an old scratched up 45.

Dang Trace, what are you doing?

And then they started looping with Lynette's lecture...

You don't know him...What you have is not real... It's an illusion...

Dang, Trace, what are you doing?
It's an illusion...
What are you doing?
After listening to that mix run through my mind for most of the night, I began to realize that was a very good question. What *was* I doing?

In an attempt to shut my brain up, I tried contacting Jaylen. I hoped that hearing his voice would clear up any confusion I had and help all this make sense to me, but after waiting ten minutes for a response to my text he simply typed back, "With the missus. I'll talk to you tomorrow."

Having gotten so little sleep the night before, I literally dragged myself out of bed and threw on a pair of pink sweats so I could drive over to mama's house. Jazzmine's birthday was in a couple of weeks and we were getting together to plan her celebration.

It didn't take longer than 15 minutes for me to get frustrated and ready to walk out of the door. Mama was trying to plan an extravaganza to rival every other five-year old's in the city. Clowns, magicians, Bouncy Houses... there wasn't anything that she'd left off her list.

"Mama, are you kidding?" I asked incredulously and in an elevated tone. "You know I can't afford all that. Hell, I can barely afford *any* of that!"

"I told you over the phone that I am going to help you pay for it. Besides, Jazz is already so excited about everything; especially the clown."

"You already told her!" I fussed. "Why did you do that? Now I am going to look like the bad guy when I tell her that I don't have the money to get all that stuff for her!"

"Didn't you just hear me say that I am going to handle most of it? What is the problem?" Mama yelled.

"The problem," I yelled back, "is that I don't want your help! It's bad enough that you and Ma-Me are practically raising her for me as it is! I am trying my best to make a comfortable life for me and my child, working my behind off to try and support her. The least you can do is let me pay for my own child's birthday party."

With that statement, mama gave me a look that let me know that I was close to crossing the line. Made me feel like I was thirteen again.

"Listen up, little girl," she said in a quiet tone. "The first thing that you are going to do is watch your volume with me. I don't care how grown you are, don't ever forget, *I'm* the mama.

Second, don't make it sound as if Ma-Me and I are taking over the raising of your child. You leave Jazzmine here all the time because you want to, not because we are begging you to."

"I'm sorry mama," I interjected. "You're right. I shouldn't have gotten loud. And I am not trying to make it seem as if you are Ma-Me are taking over. I'm just frustrated sometimes that I can't have her with me all the time."

"Tracey, we all choose the life we want to lead."

"You're right," I conceded. "Mama, I am well aware of every mistake that I've made. I know that I've made choices that made my life a little harder than it had to be, but hindsight is twenty-twenty. Now I'm just trying to find a way to make the best out of what could have become a bad situation.

I wish that I made more money. I wish that I didn't have to work two jobs and can still barely buy Jazzy the things that she needs. I wish that I had a husband, and Jazz had a father that we could both rely on."

"Hell, if wishes were fishes then the Mississippi would be full and everybody would have a po'boy on their plate," mama declared.

I shook my head at her, trying to figure out what in the world she was trying to get at with that statement, but before I was able to decipher her ridiculousness, she pulled me into a tight hug.

"Listen, baby, I know that you are doing your best. Ma-Me and I don't mind helping with Jazzmine one bit. As a matter of fact, we love it. You know that little girl is our heart. And though I was not happy with the timing and the circumstances of her appearance in our lives please don't think for a moment that I would change one bit of it, because I wouldn't. I just don't want you to make the same mistakes that I made."

My ears perked up. I had never heard mama talk about ever making any mistakes, especially when it came to raising her kids.

"After your father left, I spent so much time trying to make sure that you and your sister had all the things that you wanted, all the things that your friends had, that I nearly worked myself to the bone. I didn't get one thin dime from your father so I had to be the head and the tails. The only problem was, working so much had me missing out on valuable time that I could have been spending with my children. I had the best of intentions, just like you, but the bottom line is, I will never be able to get those moments back."

"I know mama. And believe me, now that I'm a parent I understand the sacrifices that you had to make."

"Yeah, you understand now, but think about how you felt when you were a child. You weren't thinking about the fact that the mortgage had to be paid and food had to be bought. All you knew was I wasn't there when you wanted me to be. I know that is not the childhood that you want Jazzmine to remember."

"You're right, mama, as usual," I said, realizing, probably for the first time, just how beautiful my mother was, both inside and out.

"I'm going to get it together. I promise."

Verse forty: congratulations

Kenya and I were sitting across the table from one another at The G Spot, having a late lunch. I reached into my purse and pulled out the wedding invitation, sliding it over to her without saying a word. Anyone walking pass could take one look at me and see that I was a woman who was seriously pissed off.

"Mrs. Katherine Boudreaux cordially invites you to the wedding of her daughter, Valarie Marie Boudreaux to Mr. Jean-Paul Baptiste," she read aloud, and then she looked up at me and asked, "so...what's the problem?"

"What's the problem?" I asked, looking at her with eyes practically popping out of their sockets. "Kenya, how can you sit over there and ask me what is the problem? My ex-best friend and the guy who stole my virginity, who got me pregnant and left me to figure all this mess out on my own, are getting married. To one another! That is the problem!"

Kenya took a bite of her lobster salad and then asked, "Ok, didn't you say that Valarie has never been a true friend to you?"

I nodded.

"And didn't you say that JP was an arrogant, perverted, snake in the grass and that you wouldn't give him five minutes of your time if he was the last man on earth?"

This time I verbalized my agreement. "Yes."

"Well," she returned after eating a second forkful of food. "Again, I ask, what is the problem?"

I took a moment to answer, wanting to analyze my feelings and choose my words carefully. Finally, I admitted, "I guess I'm just bitter, and probably even a little jealous."

Kenya looked at me curiously, but gave me a moment to elaborate.

"I don't care about the two of them being together, not at all. If they are the same lying and conniving people that they were when I knew them then I am sure that they are going to live unhappily ever after. They deserve one another. But I guess I'm jealous because Valarie chose him over me. All those years I thought that we were the best of friends. I thought that she had my back just as much as I had hers and then she turns around and does something so dirty. I just never understood how she could do something so low down to me."

I went on. "I wonder if she had been planning on being with him the whole time. I think that if I had

173

some closure, just a few answers, then I could finally let all this go for once and for all."

"Yeah, closure would be nice," Kenya said, "but we don't always get what we want, do we?"

"Tell me about it," I agreed, taking a sip of iced tea.

I looked over at Kenya, my home girl, in her red and white polka dot sundress and her natural hair sprouting curls going in a million different directions, and I felt so blessed to have a friend that I could love and trust completely.

Kenya and I finished our meal and were sharing an absolutely sinful bread pudding soaked in a whisky sauce when Greg sidled up to our table.

"Greg! Hey!" I said with my spoon still lingering in my mouth. "I was hoping that you would be here today. I wanted you to meet my friend Kenya."

"I'm always here; you know I have no life." Greg chuckled and reached out to shake Kenya's hand. "Kenya, good to meet you," he said.

"The pleasure is all mine," Kenya said and giggled like she was back in grade school. I rolled my eyes at her silliness. I knew exactly what she was going to say as soon as Greg left.

Greg had barely taken two steps towards the kitchen when Kenya started in on me.

"Sista-girl, are you crazy? How can you keep a man that fine in the 'friend zone'?"

"Yeah, Greg is fine," I admitted, "but I don't know. I don't want to do anything to hurt him like I have in the past."

"Why do you think you might hurt him?" Kenya asked quizzically.

I shrugged my shoulders in the form of an answer, and then she hit me with the zinger.

"Does it have anything to do with the man that I saw you with in Baton Rouge?"

I almost fell out of my seat!

I had wanted to tell Kenya about my relationship with Jaylen for a while, but every time I would fix my lips to tell her the words got stuck in my throat. Kenya is my girl, my sister, my ace boon coon. Because she was all these things to me, I knew her inside out. I knew that she would be disappointed in me, and she didn't waste any time letting me know how much.

"Ladies and gentlemen, let's give it up one more time for Ms. Tracey Dubois!"

I finished up my last set at Harrah's, and practically leaped from the stage and into my honey's arms.

Jaylen was waiting in the audience for me, looking scrumptious in tan slacks, a cream button down shirt with a loosely knotted stripped tie. I couldn't help fantasizing, as I was singing someone else's hit songs, the things that I wanted him to do to me with that tie.

When we finally made it back to my apartment, we were making out so fast and furiously that we barely made it through the door. All the advice and admonitions that Lynette and Greg had given me, and all the names that Kenya had called me, were completely out of the window. The only thing that mattered at that moment was Jaylen Baker and the incredible way that he made me feel.

We crossed the threshold with our tongues deep in one another's mouths, fingers intertwined in one another's hair. "Now...right now," I moaned, unknotting his tie.

He untangled his fingers from my hair and ran his hands up the spine of my back, trying to unzip my dress. I redirected his hand to my side and before I could let out another moan, I felt my dress fall in a silk heap around my ankles.

"You are so damn sexy," he murmured, his eyes taking in every inch of me. I took a moment to bask in the fact that I hadn't second guessed my idea to go commando style under my body-hugging black dress.

Hearing his compliment got me more aroused, as if that was even possible. I lunged for his zipper and in an instant, I had my hands wrapped around the evidence of his desire for me.

"Tracey, what are you trying to do to me?" He muttered.

"Love you," I whispered. "I am trying to love you."

"You do, my baby. I can tell you do. Let me show you how much I love you back," he said, as he turned me around and bent me over my living room sofa.

Verse forty-one: superstitions

I was in such a good mood after being so thoroughly satisfied by Jaylen that I walked into mama's house whistling. Lord, what did I do that for?

"Girl, what is the matter wit' you, coming in dis house with dat damn whistling! Don't you know its bad luck to whistle in the house?"

Many people who are not from my fair city have a crazy preconceived notion that we New Orleanians practice voodoo. That is a crazy fallacy. I'm not saying that there aren't a weirdo or two who dibble and dabble into witchcraft or the occult, but I've lived in New Orleans all my life and I have never encountered anyone I know burying someone's underwear in their backyard, or collecting strands of hair out of a hairbrush to place a hex on anyone.

As religious as Ma Me is (when it suits her needs) she would never consider anything as blasphemous as voodoo. But she is superstitious as hell. Every time I turn around, she is spewing some new superstition. Don't sweep anyone's feet or they will go to jail, never place a hat on top of the bed; and now, apparently, I can't whistle in the house because evidently it would bring me bad luck. What she didn't realize was that I was on such a high after my mind blowing night with Jaylen that I could smash a mirror while walking under a ladder on Friday the thirteenth, and I still would feel nothing less than lucky and loved.

"My left eye been twitching all morning, and now you walk in dis house wit dat whistling. I must be 'bout to make my maker for sure," Ma Me murmured as she walked down the hall to her room.

Jazzmine and I were sitting Indian style on the floor playing a game of Candy Land when my phone started ringing. Terrence Trent D'arby's jam 'Dance Little Sister' let me know that Lynette was calling. I stretched my legs out and held out a finger to Jazzmine, letting her know that I needed a minute to take the call.

"Hey, Tootie, what's going on?"

"Not much, that's why I'm calling. It's been awhile since we've gotten together. What do you think about meeting Kenya and me over at the House of Blues tonight?"

"I don't think that Kenya wants to be around me right now," I said.

"Yeah, she told me that you guys exchanged words the other day."

"Well she told you wrong because *we* didn't exchange words. She was throwing words at me. I was the one sitting there with my mouth wide open."

"I'm sure that it wasn't that bad."

"Yeah, it kinda was. I knew that Kenya had strong views on infidelity, but dang, I didn't expect her to come out of a bag like that on me."

"Trace, you know that Kenya loves you. She's just worried about you, that's all. Besides, you know how hard it was for her when her father left her mother for another woman. It devastated her, and I'm sure it's shaped her views on the subject."

"I love her too, but Kenya needs to realize that not everything is black and white. There are about a billion shades of gray in the middle of this mess.

The silence that I received from Lynette on the other end of the line let me know that she was about as color blind as Kenya on the subject.

Jazzmine and I finished our game and had an early dinner together. Before leaving I gave my daughter her ritual four kisses; one on her forehead, one on each cheek, and one on her nose, and told her that I loved her more than the stars in the sky and more than the sand on the beach. I was walking towards the door when I heard her call behind me, "Hey...mommy."

"Yes, sweetie?" I asked.

"Nothing," she answered, smiling her angelic smile at me. "I just wanted to tell you that you're cute."

I walked back towards her and scooped her up in my arms. "You're cute, too, you little munchkin," I said, tickling her belly while she squealed with delight.

I couldn't believe how close my relationship with Greg was getting. In just a few short weeks. I had begun to look forward to our daily phone conversations and occasional outings. I knew that his feelings for me were slightly different than my feelings towards him, but I was careful not to say or do anything that would be misleading to him. I enjoyed his company and valued his friendship, but Jaylen Baker owned my entire heart, even if I didn't own his.

"I'm trying to figure out how a person could live in the N.O. her whole life and still not know how to properly eat crawfish."

Greg and I were chilling on the Lakefront, eating crawfish and drinking Heinekens. The weather was perfect for late August. There was a slight breeze, stirring up murky waves in the muddy Mississippi and, for a change; the humidity level was relatively low so just about everyone and their mama were out there, playing loud music and toasting one last time to the end of summer.

"You have to suck the head. That's where all the flavor is," he said, practically inhaling the mudbug.

I started laughing. "That's just like a man. Always trying to get a lady to suck the head," I said, tossing a shell in the direction of a huge pile of previously discarded shells.

"Alright, lady," Greg laughed back. "Don't steer this conversation in a direction that you're not ready to go."

I chuckled at his brashness and quickly decided that he had a point. I knew that I had to tow a fine line while hanging out with Greg. No sexy or romantic talk. I decided to change the subject.

"So, you'll never believe what Jaylen said to me last night," I started.

Greg stood up and started cleaning up our mess. I could tell by the look on his face that he was angry with me, but I couldn't figure out what I had done.

"What?" I asked, staring up at him. "Why'd you turn so cold all a sudden?"

"Look, Tracey," he said, sitting back down on the bench next to me. "Though I don't understand your choices I have to respect the fact that you're a grown woman and you are doing what you want to do."

"You just don't understand," I interrupted, but Greg cut me off.

"You asked me what was wrong with me. Do you want to hear what I have to say or not?"

"Yes, of course I do," I answered, wondering once again where this aggressive and self-assured Gregory came from.

"The other night at the restaurant I put it all out there for you. I told you how I feel about you, how I've always felt for you. It's apparent that you don't feel the same for me and I must accept that. Of course, I would like more, but if all you can offer me is your friendship then I'll take what I can get. But what's not about to happen is you trying to turn me into one of your girlfriends."

"I'm not trying to turn you into my girlfriend," I muttered, attempting to defend myself, but Greg held up his hand to cut me off and continued his speech.

"I don't want to hear about what he says to you, and I sure as hell don't want to hear about what he does to you. Personally, I think that he is a jerk to keep stringing you along when he knows that he has no intentions of leaving his wife for you.

So, you asked what is wrong with me. What's wrong with me is the fact that the woman that I am in love with is in love with someone else; someone who doesn't even come close to deserving her. Does that answer your question?"

I shook my head yes and didn't say anything else.

There was nothing else to say.

Verse forty-two: don't want to be a fool

It seemed like every time I felt like I was getting one step ahead with Jaylen something would happen that took me two steps back. He never came straight out and said it but he started hinting around about leaving his wife and starting a new life with me. I almost couldn't breathe when he said things like that. The idea of going to bed and then waking up with Jaylen everyday sounded too good to be true.

But right when I'd begin to think that my happily ever after was about to be more than just a fairytale Jaylen would turn around and do something like what he did tonight, calling me at the last minute with some flimsy excuse as to why he couldn't come and see me, and made me realize that I would probably never be anything other than what I already am: the side chick.

I caught an unwanted glance of myself in my full-length mirror. I looked some kind of stupid sitting on the edge of my bed, all decked out in white skinny jeans, a pale-yellow silk blouse, and nude colored stilettos. All dressed up with nowhere to go.

I stood up and pushed my auburn-streaked bob back behind my ear. The way I saw it, I had two choices: I could either sit around feeling sorry for myself, or I could figure out a way to salvage my night. I opted for the latter.

"Hey, Greg, what are you up to tonight?" I asked as soon as he picked up the phone.

"Actually, not much," he said. I could practically hear his smile seeping through the phone. "I have a rare night off, so I was going to put together a quick meal and probably park myself in front of the television. Why, are you interested in joining me?"

"Well," I said, pretending like I was considering his offer, when I had already decided that I was up to anything he suggested. After all, nothing could have been worse than sitting around torturing myself with possible reasons that Jaylen could have had to cancel on me. "it's not the best sounding offer that I've ever received, but I *guess* I could join you for dinner and a movie," I joked.

"Fantastic, I'll be by to pick you up in about thirty minutes."

"No, it doesn't make sense for you to come all the way over here. Just give me directions to your place and I'll be there in a little while."

I jotted down the directions on a notepad next to my phone, grabbed my purse, and locked my door behind me before I had a chance to change my mind.

I pulled in front of the address Greg had given me and had to double check to make sure that I was in the right place. 1215 Coliseum Street, yep, I was in the right place.

The house was nothing like what I pictured Greg to live in. It was a turn of the century salmon colored two-story Victorian in the heart of the Garden District with wrap around porches on both levels. There was even a wooden swing nestled underneath a huge magnolia tree in the front yard. Very relaxing and quaint, and very unlike the workaholic Greg that I knew. I rang the doorbell to see what other surprises Greg had in store for me.

Greg's eyes lit up when he saw me. The very response that I was hoping to get from Jaylen.

"Hey, beautiful, you're just in time," he said as he let me in. He was wearing well worn-in faded Levi's and a Saints t-shirt that broadcast the fact that he was no stranger to the gym. Looking so good that I had to mentally remind myself that he was in the 'friend zone'.

"Dinner's almost ready," he said, seemingly oblivious to the fact that I was almost drooling and it had nothing to do with what was in those pots.

We walked down a long foyer into the family room. I wasn't sure what Greg had cooking but it sure smelled like Heaven.

"Did you have a hard time finding the place?"

"No, your directions were spot on, but I'll tell you, I was surprised when I pulled up in front of your house," I admitted. "It's not at all what I expected."

Greg started laughing. His trademark sound that seemed to rise from deep in his belly.

"I know. I get that all the time. I bought this house as a surprise for my mother, but I guess the surprise was on me. Right after the closing, I blindfolded her and took her to what I considered her dream house. She took one look at it and told me 'thanks, but no thanks'."

I started laughing along with him.

"Are you serious?

"Yep. Apparently, she loved her little house in Picayunne, Mississippi and had no desire to pack up and move into this 'great big ole mansion'- her words, not mine. So, I've been here ever since."

I shook my head and chuckled. I would have been ticked off had I presented my mama with such an expensive and thoughtful gift only to have her say 'no thanks'. Greg was the most easy-going person I knew. I could picture him now, giving his mom a kiss on the cheek and saying, "oh well, I tried."

Greg took me on a tour of the house, which was more impressive inside than it was from the outside, if that was even possible. We ended our tour in the kitchen, which looked everything like I imagined a chef's kitchen would look like. A huge sub-zero refrigerator took up almost half of one wall and the rest of the appliances were top-of-the line, restaurant quality.

"Greg, this place is amazing!" I said.

"Thanks. It's not what I would have picked out for myself, but I have to admit, it's starting to grow on me. Too much house for just one person, though." The look that he gave me seemed to bore deep to my soul.

Had me feeling like I was standing in front of him butt naked.

I cleared my throat and changed the subject.

"So, what's for dinner?"

"Well, I remembered how much you enjoyed the crab cakes so I made a couple of them as an appetizer. And for our entrée I prepared blackened redfish and crawfish etouffee with grilled asparagus."

"Dang, Greg," I said, "You were able to pull all that together in thirty minutes? I'm seriously impressed."

"Baby girl, cooking is what I do. I could have put this meal together in my sleep," he joked.

"Alright Mr. Cocky," I teased.

"No, all jokes aside, I had most of it prepped before you called. I was just happy that I would have someone to help me eat all this food. I'm especially happy that that someone is you."

I willed myself not to blush and reminded myself, yet again, of the Biz Markie song, that Greg was 'Just a Friend'.

Greg behaved himself throughout dinner. He didn't say anything else to make me uncomfortable. Instead he shared with me his vision for the restaurant and his plans for expansion. He also told me about an organization that he is a part of, called, Real Men Cook, that features men- professional chefs as well as amateur home cooks, volunteering to cook for and serve in their communities. His face lit up as he talked about his work. It was evident that Greg put his heart and soul in everything that he decides to do.

I wasn't sure if it was the wine or the conversation, but whatever it was had me feeling all funny inside. I took a shaky bite of fish and then Greg reached over and wiped my bottom lip with his thumb. "You missed," he teased.

'Lord, I need to get up out of here before I start to blur these lines,' I thought to myself.

I wiped my mouth with the linen napkin that was resting on my lap and started to stand. "Greg, thank you so much for dinner but I need to get going."

Greg also stood. "You can't leave yet. We haven't even had dessert. I know you can't say no to Bananas Foster."

He was right. I couldn't. Greg prepared our dessert in his outdoor kitchen. He even made a big show of lighting the bananas and rum and creating a big, dramatic flame, before pouring the sauce over vanilla ice cream. I clapped as if I was watching an act from the UniverSoul Circus and he grinned like a little boy and dipped into a deep bow.

We took our dessert over to a small bistro table that was situated next to an in-ground lap pool and heated spa. Dark purple bougainvillea crept up the brick wall bordering his property and the air smelled of mint and gardenias.

"Greg, this is absolutely beautiful. I could live out here," I gushed.

"Well, that's a thought, isn't it?" He smiled, and then quietly stood and started clearing away our dishes.

"Let me do that. Please, it's the least I can do," I said as I removed the dishes from his hands and walked through the French doors, back inside the house. I made my way to the kitchen and began filling his sink up with sudsy water. I could hear Greg come in behind me but he must have stopped off at his home theater system because Rachelle Ferrell's angelic voice came piping through his sound system.

I smiled when Greg finally came in to join me. "Great choice," I complimented his taste in music. "Rachelle Ferrell is one of my favorites."

"She's good, but not as good as you."

"Okay, now I know that you had too much wine," I chuckled and kept my head down as if I expected to find the secrets of the universe inside of those bubbles.

Greg picked up a towel and began drying the dishes that I'd washed. He was quiet for a minute and then he said, "Tracey, you know, it's amazing to me that you have no idea how incredible you are."

"Greg..."

"You are. And I'm not just talking about the singing. Of course, you take my breath away every time you open your mouth to sing, but I'm talking about everything else about you. Your poise and self-confidence."

He paused, and then said, "I know how difficult it was for you when you got pregnant with Jazz. I saw the way the people at church and school were ostracizing you, but just like with everything else you do, you handled it with strength and class."

Greg's words were so tender that I didn't know how to process them. He said that I handled my pregnancy with strength, but I'll tell you, strong is the last thing that I felt at that time. Half the time I could barely eat or sleep at night. And though Lynette and Kenya called what JP did to me 'date rape' I couldn't seem to make my mind turn off the slideshow of events leading up to "the incident": The sexy makeover, the way I flirted with him, letting him kiss and grind all over me. I couldn't help wondering if maybe JP was right. Maybe I did ask for it.

Greg reached over and wiped my face with his fingertips. Now where did those tears come from?

"I'm sorry, I did not mean to make you cry," he said.

"No, it's not your fault. It's just that I tried to bury all that so deep, it just hurts when it floats back up to the surface, that's all."

Greg took my hand and walked me over to his living room sofa. He handed me a tissue and once he got me situated, he said, "I have a confession to make."

I gazed at him until he was ready to continue. Finally, he said, "You know, I beat myself up about letting you go off with JP that night. I feel responsible. I should have insisted that you let me take you home that night."

I couldn't believe that Greg felt that way.

"No, Greg, you have no reason to beat yourself up about that. You remember how hard-headed and determined I was back then. There was nothing that you could have said that would have changed things."

He seemed to think about that for a minute and then he said, "Every time I think about the way you looked when you got in my car that night, I want to go back and beat that joker's behind all over again."

I chuckled, then realized what he'd just said.

"Wait a minute, what do you mean all over *again*?"

"You didn't know? As soon as I dropped you off, I went straight back to Sister Baptiste's house looking for JP. He wasn't home when I got there, but about ten minutes later he pulled into the driveway. As soon as he got out of the car, I confronted him about what he did to you."

"Are you serious?" I asked. I was amazed that I was just hearing about this.

"Yeah, I'm serious. He told me some cocky mess about you asking for it and then I lost it! I attacked his ass!"

I started cracking up thinking about the chubby, nerdy Greg that he used to be trying to beat somebody up on my behalf.

"So, did you win the fight?" I asked.

"Hell, naw. He whupped my out of shape ass." Greg's laugh seemed to take up every inch of the room. "That's okay, though. I bet he can't take me now," he said, flexing his muscles.

I continued laughing and reached over and gave him a hug. "I can't believe that you did that for me."

He got all serious then. Looked me straight in the eye and said, "Tracey, don't you know by now that there is nothing that I wouldn't do for you."

Verse forty-three: papa was a rolling stone

I put my hands on my hips and looked at my sister as if she had just grown a second head. "Are you crazy? This is gonna take all night! I thought you said that you only had a few things left to pack!"

When I promised Lynette that I would help her move into a larger apartment I didn't think that it would be an all-day job. From the look of all the boxes and junk that she still had lying all over the place looked like we would be here all day and all night! I didn't think so!

"Girl, stop being so dramatic and throw those sweaters into the box! If you weren't stopping every five minutes to check your phone we could have been done by now.

She was right, to an extent. I was waiting on a text from Jaylen to find out if he would be able to sneak out tonight. So far, no good. Looked like it was gonna be just me, Lynette, and this mountain of boxes towering in front of us. I folded a few more sweaters and placed them inside the box, but not before keeping a couple of the cuter ones out for myself.

I taped the box shut and began emptying out the contents of Lynette's entertainment center. I began flipping through her CD collection, trying to find something to keep me motivated to finish this boring job but wasn't having much luck. Lord, that girl has awful taste in music. Lots of bounce and rap, but nothing with substance in the bunch. I thought I taught her better than that!

"Tootie, where is all your real music?" I yelled in the direction of the kitchen where Lynette was in there wrapping glasses in old newspaper.

"What you mean, real music? *All* my music is real music! Your butt is probably looking for some old school mess like Peobo Bryson or Stephanie Mills. You better slap Lil' Wayne in there and finish packing those boxes!"

I laughed and settled for something in the middle. I decided to crank Kanye. At least he was talking about something in the middle of all that noise.

I was halfway finished with the living room when I ran across Lynette's collection of photo albums. I flipped through a few of them and got a few chuckles looking at pictures of mama and Ma-Me from back in the day. Then I saw a shot of Lynette and Ma-Me with their arms around one another. Looked like they were shopping downtown on Canal Street. Unh hunh, I knew it! Where was I when this picture was taken? And Ma-Me never held on to me like that. I knew Ma-Me liked her best!

A few pages back my face split into a wide smile when I came across a picture of Jazzmine at age three, when she wouldn't take two steps without that old tattered stuffed dog of hers. What was his name again? Oh yeah, Power Shower. Where in the world did she get that silly name from?

I placed the album in a box labeled mementos and was working my way through another album when I was interrupted by a knock at the door.

"Are you expecting someone?" I yelled to Lynette.

"Oh yeah, that's probably Kenya. Go ahead and let her in."

I rolled my eyes, but I wasn't surprised. I should have known that Lynette would invite Kenya over. Even when we were little girls Lynette would always play peacemaker with everyone in the neighborhood. She couldn't stand it when people were not getting along.

Instead of opening the door right away I stayed where I was and looked at a few more pictures. Let her behind stay out there for a little while.

Kenya has always been honest with me, that was one of the main things that I love about her, but never have her words hurt me so bad. I couldn't believe that she had the nerve to call me a home wrecker.

I took a deep breath and got up to let her in. To see what else she was coming to call me.

Kenya came through the door carrying a peace offering. Chinese food, my favorite. It's hard staying mad at somebody when they smell like shrimp fried rice.

We gave each other awkward hugs but for the first time since we've been knowing one another we didn't have much to say. We were both relieved when Lynette came into the room carrying an armful of paper plates and styrofoam cups.

We set the food out on a blanket on the floor since most of Lynette's furniture had already been moved out, filled our cups to the rim with Moscato, and began digging in as if we hadn't eaten in years.

Kenya got up and changed the music, Chrisette Michele this time. We made a little small talk, mostly about Jazzmine and the things that she has been getting into, but none one of us seemed to be ready to tackle the elephant that was sitting in the room.

After a while I guess Kenya decided to put an end to the awkwardness. "Look, Trace," she blurted out, "I'm sorry about what happened. I can't say that I apologize for the way that I feel, because I still feel the same way, but I am sorry for the way that I said it. It's just that I love you like a sister and I can't stand to see you make choices that are so obviously wrong for you." She exhaled as if she was relieved to have released all that.

"Ken, I love you too. You know that. And I know that you want what's best for me. But how do you know that Jaylen isn't what's best for me."

She answered with one sentence. "Because he's married."

"But what if he got married too early? What if he only married her because she got pregnant? Are we supposed to suffer because he was trying to do the right thing?"

"No, not all," she answered, talking so fast and animatedly that her chopsticks were flying all over the place. She looked like an orchestra conductor. "But if he is such a great guy and he wants to do the right thing then he should end one relationship before he jumps into another one. It's not fair to his wife, and it's not fair to you."

I didn't know what to say to this. My egg roll felt as if it parked itself in the middle of my throat. I took a sip of wine and kept quiet.

Then Lynette threw her two cents in. Felt like they were ganging up on me. "Tracey, do you remember how we felt when mama and daddy divorced?"

I looked at her like she was crazy. "Yes, of course I remember. We both cried for days when he left."

"Do you even know *why* they got divorced?"

"I...don't...know," I dragged out my words. "I guess mama was has hating on daddy because of his singing."

"No, how about mama was hating on daddy because of the woman that he was sneaking out with when he claimed that he was out singing."

I was not ready for the direction that this conversation was going in. Sure, I was pissed at daddy for deserting our family and not being there when Lynette and I needed him, but the thought of him leaving mama, leaving all us, for another woman was more than I could bear.

I barely recognized my voice when I spoke again. "Who told you that? Mama?"

"No, actually I overheard a conversation that she and Ma-Me were having when they thought we were asleep."

I took another gulp of my wine. My temples were starting to throb, that always happened when I drank too much, too fast; but what the hell. I took another swallow.

We stopped talking. The only sound in the room was the sound of our sipping and Chrisette Michele singing about her epiphany. Then Kenya says, "Can I play Lucy for a minute?"

"Who?" Lynette and I asked in unison.

"Lucy... you know the little chick from Charlie Brown. That one that pretended she was a psychiatrist and was always giving out advice for five cents, or some mess like that."

Lynette laughed and I shook my head yes, but I was pretty sure that I already knew what advice she had for me. The same thing that she'd been saying since she found out about him: stop seeing Jaylen.

Instead she said, "I'll start with myself." She cleared her throat and then she proclaimed, "My daddy left, and because of that, I suffer from insecurity and low self-worth. I find happiness in the bottom of a bag of potato chips. I have a hard time trusting men, but I am letting go and I am moving on!"

She raised her cup and clicked it against ours.

"Now your turn," she said, motioning towards Lynette.

Lynette hesitated and then she said, "My daddy left and because of that I hardly ever date. I say things like I'm too busy or I'm too tired but in the back of my mind I'm thinking that it doesn't make sense getting close to someone because they are probably are going to do something to hurt me or let me down."

"And..." Kenya prompted.

"And I am letting go and I am moving on!" Lynette added. She raised her cup for her toast and then she said, "Alright, Tracey, it's on you."

197

I took a deep breath. I didn't want to do this. They just sat there, looking at me expectedly, so I mumbled, "My daddy left... and because of that...,"

I stopped. I wasn't sure how to complete this statement. I'm sure that my father's absence left a huge hole in my heart and went a long way towards shaping the person that I've become but I never really sat down to think it. How has it affected me? What would I have done differently had I had grown up wrapped in the security of the blanket of a father's love?

"I can't," I whispered and started crying. The girls scooted closer to me and we held each other tight. The love that was radiating from them seemed to give me strength. Finally, I was ready to speak.

"My daddy left, and because of that... because of that I am attracted to older men. Men that are not always available, or who do not deserve me."

I drained the last of my drink and slurred, "And I'm letting go and I'm moving on."

Verse forty-four: you made a fool of me

I said that I was letting go of daddy, I didn't say that I was ready to let go of Jaylen. Apparently, he was trying to let go of me.

He stood me up. I mean this time, seriously, straight up, left me hanging. Had me sitting in a restaurant all by myself looking like *Boo Boo the Fool*. I called him about a half a dozen times but his phone kept sending me straight to voicemail. I was livid!

Now it was my turn to ignore him. I sat on the edge on my bed, listening to the phone ring and ring. I had to will myself not to answer. I was dying to find out what happened; what could have possibly caused him to treat me so callously, but my pride would not let me answer the phone. I wanted him to know what it felt like to be snubbed and disregarded.

My girl Chaka was on my CD player singing about risking it all and going through the fire for her man. I grabbed the remote control and turned the volume all the way down to zero. Shit, I was getting tired of running through fires, getting my ass all burned up.

I desperately wanted to call Greg and get his take on these latest developments, but he had made it abundantly clear the other night at the lake that he was not interested in being my relationship guru. As a matter of fact, he had been noticeably distant lately. I was hoping that he would be at Jazzmine's birthday party later this afternoon so we could talk and get back to the way things used to be between us.

The phone rang again. This time, after the fifth ring, I couldn't resist. I reached out and grabbed it off my nightstand.

"Tracey, I know you are angry with me, but please, just let me explain," Jaylen said.

"Jaylen, whatever you have to say to me you could have told me the other night at the restaurant. Oh wait...you couldn't tell me at the restaurant because you never showed up at the damn restaurant, did you!" I yelled into the receiver and then slammed the phone back on its base.

I felt pleased with myself. Glad that I had remained strong and had given Jaylen a piece of my mind; but then I suddenly began to question myself. Perhaps I shouldn't have hung up on him. I should have listened to his explanation, maybe something horrible happened, keeping him from coming to me or calling me.

Two minutes later the phone began to ring again. This time I picked it up on the second ring. I held the receiver to my ear and didn't say a word.

"Baby, please don't hang up," Jaylen begged. "Just give me a chance to tell you what happened."

I sighed and steadied myself for yet another round of his excuses.

"I was walking out the door, leaving to meet you at Mandina's, when Linda started feeling sick. She was complaining of stomach cramps and feeling dizzy. At first, I thought that she would feel better after eating soup and getting some rest and I would still be able to meet you, but then she started feeling worse. I wound up having to take her to the emergency room."

"Unh hunh," I muttered. "And how is Linda now?" I asked, not really caring about his answer.

"She's much better now," he responded.

And then I took a stab in the dark. "And how is the baby?"

Crickets. Jaylen didn't utter one word into the phone.

"How is the baby, Jaylen?" I slowly repeated.

I heard him inhale and then he said, "The baby is fine."

I was so furious that I could barely see straight. I looked at the phone, which was still in my hand, as if it were some foreign object. Then I threw it clean across the room, smashing it against the door jamb.

That dirty dog! All the time that he was with me, loving on me, he was apparently also loving on his wife. Making a baby with her!

The rational part of me knew that I had no right to be mad at Jaylen. It was his prerogative if he wanted to have a baby with his wife. And though he claimed that he loved me, I had to remind myself that he'd never actually promised me happily ever after.

But me, Jaylen, and rational were never exactly words that were written on the same page; and though I had no right to be mad, I was actually mad as hell!

Verse forty-five: angel of mine

The phone call from Jaylen put me in a dark place, left me sobbing and feeling like crap all morning, but the phone call from my daughter brought me back.

"Mama, where are you?" Jazzmine asked as soon as I answered the phone. "My party has already started. Everyone is here but you."

"Oh, Jazzy baby," I said, wiping tears from my eyes. Remembering, for the first time in a long time, what was important in my life. All the things that I let fall by the wayside in my pursuit of Jaylen and his love. "I'm sorry. Mommy will be there in twenty minutes," I promised her.

I quickly washed my face, ran a brush through my hair and grabbed Jazzmine's wrapped gift off the kitchen table.

As I was driving to mama's house, I couldn't help reflecting on the first time I'd laid eyes on my angel.

"It's a girl! A beautiful baby girl," Dr. Stephens said as she placed the screaming, bloody bundle in my outstretched arms.

I looked down at her, crying as if she was trying to sing a lullaby to herself, and even through all the gook and the noise I could see that the doctor was right. My baby was beautiful. A perfect gift from God, despite the circumstances of her conception and birth.

I'd heard people say that once you have a baby you forget all about the pain of childbirth. As I was going through all the pushing and the hollering and the cursing, I had a hard time believing that to be true. But the first time I laid eyes on my daughter, my precious Jazzmine Elizabeth, I knew that they had spoken the truth. In that one instant, I'd completely forgotten about the agony of contractions that seemed as if they were tearing my body in two. I'd forgotten about the pain and the shame that JP had inflicted on me. I'd even forgotten about the looks that I caught glances of as I waddled down the school hallways or sang in church with a belly that was practically bursting through my choir robe.

I forgot about everything but the unfaltering love that I felt for the little girl lying in my arms, whose life I was now completely responsible for.

I couldn't help but shed a few tears as I drove to my mama's house. But this time I was not crying because of Jaylen's indiscretions. This time I was crying because I felt the need to cleanse myself of all the bad choices that I'd made and start making room for some good ones.

As I turned onto mama's street I began cursing under my breath. She'd done exactly what I asked her not to do. She'd gone all out and planned a party that I couldn't possibly pay for. There were pink and lavender balloons tied to the stair banister and a huge sign announcing "A Princess Party" was taped to the mailbox. Kids were running all around the yard and I could spot the top of a bouncy house in the backyard.

Mama must have gone through her phone book and invited everyone that she even vaguely knew. Cars were tightly parked on both sides of the street as far down as I could see.

I slowed down to try to figure out where I could park and then I noticed Jazzmine sitting on the edge of the stairs; looking like Lynette and I used to look as we sat on Ma Me steps waiting for mama to come and pick us up on Friday nights after work. Those nights right after the divorce when she hardly ever showed up at all.

Our eyes met at the same time and a slow smile spread across her face. I watched her stand up, and before I knew it, she was darting between two parked cars, trying to get to me.

"No, Jazzmine!" I screamed, but the windows were up and there was no way she could possibly hear me. She also didn't see the car that was speeding towards her. The car that was racing to end my baby's life on the very day that she'd been gifted to me, only five short years earlier.

Verse forty-six: tears in heaven

If one more person tells me that they know how I feel I will scream. Just totally fuckin' scream! How in the hell could they possibly know how I feel when *I* don't even know how I feel.

My emotions are all over the place. A crazy ass fusion of feelings that I can't even name nor describe. One moment might have me feeling as if, with the help of God and my family, I could possibly get through this agony. But right when I start to try and marinate in those feelings everything changes. The reality of it hits me all over again and the pain is so intense and overbearing that it feels physical.

From top to bottom my whole-body hurts, as if I was the one who was struck by a car and tossed three feet in the air before landing crumpled and broken on the sidewalk, and not my precious baby.

But most of all I feel as if this all must be a dream. Some type of crazy nightmare that I am going to eventually wake up from. I mean, surely this couldn't be real. Surely that couldn't have been me sitting in a funeral home picking out a white lacquered coffin with a pink satin lining for my child. Surely, I'm not the person perusing through photo albums looking for the perfect picture of Jazzmine to have enlarged to place next to her casket. And surely, straight up for sure, I can't be the person who wakes up, screaming every night, aching for my baby and the chance to hold her in my arms at least one more time.

The weather on the morning of the funeral was foggy and gray; a perfect representation of all our feelings. I woke up early, after yet another nightmare, and noticed that at some point throughout the night mama had crawled into bed besides me. Seeing her sleeping next to me made me think about the night that she found out that I was pregnant and instead of cursing me out and throwing me out of the house as I thought she would, she crawled into my bed and promised me that everything would be alright.

Well, despite her drunken proclamation and her best intentions, everything was not alright. It wasn't even close to being alright.

I slipped out of bed as quietly as I could, wanting to spare her from the heartbreaking reality that was waiting for her as soon as she opened her eyes.

I padded through the house in a pair of stripped slipper socks and one of my old nightgowns, grateful for the peace and quiet. It seemed as if ever since "it" happened, people were near and around me every time I turned around. Bringing me tea, trying to force feed me soup and sandwiches, rubbing my back and telling me to trust in God, that He has a plan and He is never wrong.

I knew that they meant well, but I wanted to tell them to take their tea and their words of wisdom and leave me the hell alone! But then, in moments when there was no one around to fuss over me and fill up the silence, I felt so overwhelmed with the enormity of my grief that the path to insanity seemed right around the corner.

Verse forty-seven: the tracks of my tears

The funeral and the repast that followed were a blur of visitors, hugs and tears. It seemed as if every person who had ever met or heard of Jazzmine had shown up to offer their condolences. I watched the procession of people as if I was floating outside of my body. I could see a woman who looked a lot like me, in a cheap pink suit, hugging and greeting people and nodding her head as if she was hearing and agreeing with what they were saying. But I couldn't connect that woman to the person that I knew I was. The person that I used to be.

As I hovered there, above the heads of the people in Mount Zion's small fellowship hall, I listened to snippets of their conversations, their sorrow, as they talked about what a special and loving girl Jazzmine is... Jazzmine was. I don't think that I will ever get used to referring to my baby in the past tense.

There were so many tears, especially from mama and Ma-Me, that instead of them comforting me, I found myself trying to comfort them. Even Lynette, who had been a pillar of strength throughout the entire ordeal eventually broke down sobbing. I wrapped my arms around her and held on as if she was a life preserver and we were both in danger of drowning.

After we both calmed down, I removed my arm from around her waist and accepted a cup of tea that Kenya was handing to me. I didn't really want it, but I knew that she was trying to be helpful and that she was dealing with an anguish of her own.

I snuck away and found a quiet spot in the corner and prayed for the day to be over. Soon I decided to quit pretending to be strong, and I began praying for my life to be over. I knew that there was no way that I could continue to go on with this huge hole in my heart.

Before I knew it, the tears were falling again. I wiped my face with my hand and then stood up to get a fresh tissue. I hadn't taken two steps before I noticed my father walking towards me. Sadness and regret were written all over his face.

"It's okay, baby girl," he crooned. "Daddy's here. Daddy's finally here."

I ran into his arms and cried a lifetime of tears.

Verse forty-eight: I want you back

I packed my bags for the fourth time and attempted to go back to my apartment. Throwing my things haphazardly into my brown leather weekender and saying a quick goodbye to everyone, this time I almost made it all the way to the front door before stopping and hesitating. A part of me wanted so badly to get away from the constant stream of phone calls and visitors and the ever present reminders of Jazzmine that were everywhere I turned in mama's house, but another part of me was worried about being alone, with only my thoughts and feelings to keep me company.

"Do you want me to go home with you?" Lynette asked. I hadn't even realized that she was standing behind me. "I could spend the night and keep you company."

"No sweetie," I answered. "I'm good. I think I need to spend some time alone."

I could tell that she was worried about me, so I added, "I'll call if I need you. I promise."

I walked through the door of my apartment and tried to ignore the smell of stale air and the feeling of loneliness that greeted me. I took in a deep breath and let it out slowly, trying to decide what to do with myself. I couldn't think of anything better to do, so I started picking up old newspapers and straightening out magazines around my living room, anything that would shut off the never-ending cacophony that was trying to get started again in my mind.

I had just finished watering the plants and was about to get started in the kitchen when the phone rang. I glanced at the caller ID and saw that it was Jaylen calling, again.

He and the rest of the crew from Baker and Brewer had shown up at the funeral. He looked at me with the saddest eyes and held me so tight but, for the life of me, I was unable to hold him back. I was no longer mad at him. As a matter of fact, I searched my heart and realized that for the first time since laying eyes on him, I didn't feel anything towards him. But I guess that wasn't saying much, because at that point I was so numb that I was barely feeling anything at all.

I listened to the phone ring and ring and then before I knew it that noise was compounded by the sound of knocking at my door. *What in the hell!* I thought I'd returned to my apartment for solitude, but apparently there was no place that I could run to for the peace that I was looking for.

I considered not answering the door, but I knew that if it was Lynette or Kenya, or even Ma-Me, they would probably commence to knocking the door down if I didn't let them in. I looked through the peephole and was surprised to see Greg looking back at me.

"I'm sorry, Greg, I'm just not in the mood..." I began before I even had the door all the way opened, but he ignored my protests and walked right past me.

"I'm not going to stay long, but I'm worried about you. I know that when I called you said that you were holding up alright, but I wanted to see for myself.

Isn't that what a *buddy* would do?" he joked, referring to our last conversation when I tried, not so subtly, to classify our relationship.

"Yes, I guess so," I said and gave him a tired smile.

Greg held my hand and walked me over to the sofa. "So, all jokes aside. How are you really?"

"I don't know," I admitted. "It all seems like a bad dream. I keep thinking I am going to wake up and Jazzmine is going to come running out of her room. But then I have to face reality and remind myself that my baby is never coming back to me. That I'll never see her, or hold her, or smell the sweet baby powder smell in the crease of her neck again."

He gave my hand a squeeze. I hadn't even realized that he was still holding on to it.

"Trace, I can't even begin to imagine what you are going through. But remember, you do not have to go through this alone. You're not the only one who loved Jazzmine. All us are hurting. Let us help you when you need the help. Even if you think you don't need the help, at least it makes us feel as if we are doing something. I don't know about everyone else, but I feel

213

so helpless. I would give anything to be able to take this pain away from you."

"I know, Greg," I said, feeling tears well up in my eyes. "I know that you are all trying to help but all this attention is starting to drive me crazy. I can't even take a breath without somebody trying to feed me, or pet me, or cry with me."

He smiled at me sheepishly. "Alright, I'm guilty. I brought you some gumbo. I came here with the intention of feeding you."

At the mention of the word gumbo, the tears that had been threatening began to fall.

"Oh no, baby, no. What's wrong?" Greg asked, pulling me closer and rubbing my back.

Hearing him mention gumbo made me think about the time that I'd spent all day cooking gumbo for Jaylen, only to have him cancel on me at the last minute. Thinking about that made me think about the fact that I missed my baby's birthday party because I was on the phone fighting with him.

Before I realized what I was doing, I was crying hysterically and telling Greg all it; everything from the gumbo, to the fight, the baby, and finally... missing Jazzmine's birthday party.

Once I got started, I couldn't stop. I felt like a bottle whose cork had just been popped. Everything came pouring out and it felt as if the enormity of the pain would destroy me.

Greg held me tight and continued to stroke my back. "It's okay, baby, it's okay. Just let it all out," he kept repeating.

"I want to take it back," I cried. "If only I could take it all back. I would do everything so differently."

I cried harder. "All the nights that I let Jazzmine sleep over at mama's house. All the times that I blew her off in order to work or spend time with Jaylen. All the church plays and highlights that I missed... I want them back, Greg! I just want my baby back!"

"I know, I know..." he crooned; and he held me and rocked me, until my sobs turned into sniffles and I felt as if I didn't have anything left to repent.

I took a deep breath and wiped my face with the back of my hand.

"I'm sorry," I said, my voice hoarse from all the confessing and crying.

"You have nothing to be sorry for, sweetheart."

"I do. You said that you didn't want to hear about me and Jaylen and I just laid all that on you. I can't even imagine what you think of me after hearing all that."

"That's different, Trace. And I didn't mean what I said. You can tell me anything. There is nothing that you can do or say to run me away. Don't you know by now how I feel about you?"

Greg lifted my chin with his fingertips, and totally ignoring my runny nose and puffy eyes, kissed me gently on my lips.

It felt so good. For just a moment, to have an emotion that was not full of pain. So, I leaned into his kiss and began to lose myself in the sensation of it.

Verse forty-nine: I'm going down

I don't know why I turned Greg away, but I did. I know that I hurt his feelings when I abruptly pulled away from his kiss and asked him to leave. I wanted to soften the blow and tell him that it wasn't him, that it was me. I just wasn't ready, or in the right frame of mind, to start something like that with him. I wanted to tell him that his friendship, and even the promise of more to come, was too important to me to risk beginning a relationship in my fragile emotional state. But I didn't. As usual, I did everything the wrong way. Sent him packing, as if *he* had done something wrong, instead of the other way around.

That annoying ass voyeur who continued to float above my body; watching, and now judging everything that I did, took one glimpse of me kissing on Greg, seeming to forget for a second that I had just buried my baby, and she turned on me big time. Made me feel not only like a piss poor parent, but an even pissier and poorer human being.

So, I decided to give in to her assessment of me.

I made my way into the kitchen, found the half bottle of Zinfandel that Essence and I hadn't polished off, and commenced to finding a liquid solution to my problems.

I woke up about five hours later, gave my alarm clock a fleeting glance, and realized that it was 8:46 in the morning. I tried to rack my brain for a minute, but couldn't seem to figure out what day it was. What did it matter anyway, Monday through Sunday, the days were all the same. The world kept spinning and my baby was still not a part of it.

I turned over and went back to sleep.

The next few days were more of the same: sleeping, drinking, crying. I tried to pull myself together; if only for the sake of my family, but the more I tried, the harder it seemed to make myself take the steps to go about my everyday routine. I hadn't been to the office or to Harrah's in over a week and just the idea of getting out of bed, taking off my tattered pj's and putting on real clothes, and trying to pretend that I was not a person who was slowly going mad, almost had me breaking out in hives.

Mitra came by one afternoon and I could see the pity in her eyes as she took in my appearance and the neglected state of my apartment. I knew that she meant well and was only trying to be a friend, as she began stacking dirty dishes into the dishwasher, but I wanted her gone so bad that it took every ounce of my willpower to not physically pick her up and deposit her on the opposite side of my door.

"So, when do you think you'll be ready to come back to work?" she asked as she grabbed the broom and began sweeping my floor. "The guys have been asking about you. They are really worried about you, especially Jaylen."

I wasn't sure if she knew about the history between Jaylen and me, but I didn't care one way or another. Jaylen had been calling every day, but I couldn't bring myself to answer his calls. I knew that what happened wasn't his fault, but the emotional part of me couldn't seem to

get past the fact that I was wasting time fighting with him about a baby that he and his wife will be holding in their arms in a few short months, when I should have been holding my own baby in my arms. For the few short moments that she had left on this earth.

"I don't know. I'm not even sure if I'm ever coming back," I replied when I noticed Mitra staring at me, waiting for an answer to her question.

"Oh, Tracey, don't say that. It won't be the same without you around there. Just take as much time as you need. I'm sure the guys will say the same thing. We'll hold everything down until you're ready to come back."

I gave her a hug and told her that I'd think about it. But as soon as I closed the door behind her, I grabbed a glass and a bottle of vodka, made my way down the hall to my bedroom, and made a conscious decision to not think about anything at all.

I thought I was dreaming when I heard banging at my front door. I couldn't detect any sunlight trying to sneak through my blinds so I assumed it was nighttime, but I was still so buzzed after drinking so much that no matter how much I tried to focus, I could not make out the time on the clock. I turned over and tried to ignore the ruckus, but whoever it was out there did not have plans of going away anytime soon. The knocking got louder and more insistent.

I stumbled my way to the front and fumbled with the lock until I was finally able to get it opened. As soon as I saw who was standing on the other side, I immediately regretted not looking through my peephole first. *JP.*

Verse fifty: what becomes of the broken hearted

That curly sandy brown hair that I was so in love with so many years ago was still atop JP's head, but time had thinned it out and he was sporting a George Jefferson like hole in his "afro".

I wanted to tell him that he needed to give up the ghost and cut it allf, and because I was in a shitty mood and full of Ciroc, I did.

"You look stupid. Cut that shit off!" was the first thing I said to my dead baby's daddy.

JP walked through the door as if he hadn't heard a word that I said. He slunk down onto the sofa and when he opened his mouth to speak, I realized that he'd probably had as much, or possible more, than I'd had to drink.

"She's gone, Tracey. Our baby is gone," he cried.

I stared at him incredulously with my mouth wide open. *'Am I in the middle of another dream?'* I wondered to myself. Surely this man is not in my house, slobbering all over my couch, crying about *our* baby being gone.

Not this man, who had not only taken advantage of my teenage naiveté and left me pregnant and alone, but the same man who also looked in my baby's face and callously stated that she wasn't his before walking away and never looking back. Somebody needed to wake me up, because I knew that I had to be dreaming.

I opened my mouth to give him a royal cursing out, but then I thought to myself, who am I to judge him for coming up short as a parent? Isn't that the same thing that I had spent the past week beating myself up about?

And then it hit me! I knew that I had a least tried. I had given Jazzmine everything that I had to give in the time that she was with me. Sure, I'd made the mistake of assuming that I would have time to make up to her for my shortcomings; but in the moment that it took me to almost curse out JP I released myself. I knew that I had done my best. And I knew that every day of the five years that she was on this earth, Jazzmine knew that I loved her.

JP had no idea about the inner dialogue I had going on with myself. He continued to sit on my sofa, crying and moaning. I walked over to him and held him.

I didn't have plans to sleep with JP. I swear I didn't. But as I comforted him and absolved him of some of his guilt regarding Jazzmine I realized that this was the man who had given me my greatest gift. And

221

because of that I could never truly hate him, no matter what he had done to me.

We sat on the couch, wrapped in each other's arms, tears blending, and before I knew it, we were kissing. And then we were doing more than kissing, and that meddling ass voyeur didn't even show her face this time. Didn't stop me from making the biggest mistake of all!

I realized the enormity of my mistake when I heard a throat clearing and looked up to see Greg looking down at me!

"I was worried about you," he said flatly. "I knocked, but the door swung open."

And then he turned around and walked out, slamming the door behind him.

Verse fifty-one: don't know why

I was sitting at the kitchen table, eating instant grits and drinking warm orange juice, listening to Norah Jones on my iPod. There was a line in her song, *Don't Know Why*, which was messing with my head. She sings about feeling as empty as a drum. Yeah, that pretty much summed me up, fit my feelings perfectly. I kept playing that part over and over until eventually I got up, dumped the juice in the sink, grabbed a Bud Light from the fridge and began making my way back to my favorite spot on the sofa.

The phone started ringing again, so I pulled it out of the socket. I was tired of talking. There wasn't anything that anyone could say to make things right for me.

About two hours later, mama, Ma-Me, Lynette, and Kenya were barging through my front door, ordering me to sit down and listen to what they had to say. I guess they called themselves having an intervention for me.

Mama plucked the beer from my hands, against my protests and started in on me.

"Tracey, you can't keep going on this way. You're not answering our phone calls, you never leave this apartment; and from the look and smell of things, it seems as if you haven't had a bath in over a week."

"So," I said, and stopped, because I couldn't think of anything else to say.

What are you supposed to say when your friends and family are in your face, telling you that you look *and smell*, a hot mess.

"I know this is a hard time for you, it's a hard time for all us," Lynette chimed in. "But Tracey, you're going to have to at least try."

And then she threw in, "Do it for, Jazzmine."

With that, I lost it!

"Don't you dare!" I spat at her. "Don't you dare throw around Jazzmine's name to try to make me feel bad, or guilty, or whatever in the hell it is that you're trying to make me feel!"

"Oh, Trace, I'm not," she rushed over to me, attempting to hug me, but I turned my body away from her. "I'm just so worried about you."

"If I hear that one more time, I am going to jump out of that window!" I threatened. "I am so tired of everybody telling me how worried they are about me. Just leave me alone! Let me get through this in my own way, in my own time!"

"We know what a sense of loss you feel," Kenya added. "And we know that the grief process is different for different people, but there are places you can go and people that you can talk to if you don't want to talk to us."

"Don't you get it," I asked, suddenly feeling exhausted even though I'd just gotten out of bed less than twenty minutes before. "I am tired of talking! Every time I turn around someone is calling my phone or knocking on my door trying to talk to me; bringing me books and pamphlets to read.

"Look at all this crap," I pointed towards a towering stack of sympathy cards and coping with loss and grief brochures that was littered across my coffee table. "I have an impressive collection going on, don't you think?"

"I even started reading through some of them," I continued. "Do you know what this one says," I asked, picking up a lavender colored brochure on the top of the pile and tossing it towards Ma-Me. "This one says that a wife who loses a husband is called a widow. A child who loses her parents is called an orphan. But, there is no word for a parent who loses a child. That's just how unnatural this is! There not even a name for what I am..."

"Lord, Jesus, please help this chile. She hurtin' Lord and she need yo arms of protection around her. Be with her through her time o' need, Sweet Jesus," Ma-Me raised her hands towards the heavens and started praying. I didn't realize that I had started crying until I felt a tear fall on my cheek.

Ma-Me grabbed my hand and uttered, "You gotta give it to God, Tracey. Ain't no way you can handle all this on yo own. You gotta give it to God. Da

225

Bible says that weeping will endure for a night, but rejoicing comes in da mornin'.

I jerked my hand from hers and felt her sharp fingernails rake across my skin. "Don't even start," I said. "I don't want to hear about rejoicing, because that's never gonna happen, and I am not in the mood to hear another word about how God has a plan and he does not give us more than we can bear. Because that's some bullshit! Do you hear me? That is some bullshit! I can't bear this! Why did he give this to me? I can't bear it!"

I began to sob.

"Don't you dare speak that blasphemy!" Ma-Me hollered at me. "Don't you know that you ain't got nothing if you ain't got faith?"

"That's just it, Ma-Me," I countered, "I *ain't* got nothing. So how 'bout that? I can say whatever I want to say because there is nothing else that he can take from me."

"Lord, Jesus, help this chile," Ma-Me wiped tears from her eyes and started mumbling another prayer.

"*You* can help me by getting out of here!" I yelled at her, at all them.

I turned back to Ma-Me.

"Why are you even here, anyway? It should have been you! Your old ass has lived a long, miserable life. Why wasn't it you?" I cried.

I heard Lynette take in a sharp intake of air and mama yell out, "Tracey!"

But Ma-Me simply walked over to me and gathered me in her arms. She pulled me down to the carpet and she held me like a baby, the way she used she used to hold me when I skinned my knee when I was a little girl. The way she used to hold Jazzmine.

"I know, chile. I know," she crooned as she rocked me from side to side. "I miss that baby as much as you do. I would lay down my life if it would bring dat lil girl back. I loved her, but I love you too."

My sobs became louder, but she kept on repeating, "Ma-Me love you, Ma-Me love you," she said over and over. Until she was sure that I believed it.

Verse fifty-two: we are family

My family, the people who have always been there with me and for me and never fail to astonish me with their unconditional love are who brought me back.

No matter what I said to them, no matter what I threw at them, both literally and figuratively, they refused to turn their back on me. They stayed until I was ready to talk, until I was ready to pray. Until I was ready to at least think about living again.

I quit both jobs, Baker and Brewer as well as Harrah's. It seemed as if I needed a new start, so I began volunteering at the hospital that mama works at. After a few weeks I realized that I felt more alive when I was at the hospital, being a help, and hopefully a blessing, to those who needed me. So, I enrolled, much to mama's delight, in nursing school.

I also put together a group of teens who loved singing as much as I did when I was their age. We traveled to children's hospitals and nursing homes singing to people in need. Mostly gospel and inspirational stuff, but every now and then I threw in a little jazz.

I was determined to make the most of the second half of my life. I know that sounds weird, coming from someone still in her twenties, but I knew that no matter how long I lived, I would always think of my life in two halves. The half with Jazzmine and the half without.

I haven't spoken to Jaylen in months. He finally took the hint and stopped calling. I guess he got tired of talking to my machine or listening to my dial tone. His last message to me was quite touching. He said that despite everything that's happened his love for me was always real and that he was sorry if he contributed in any way to the pain that I was going through.

He promised that he wouldn't try to contact me anymore, but said that he would always be there for me if I need him. His message made me think about his answer to me, at the beginning of our relationship, when I asked him what he would do if I fell in love with him. He said that he would try not to let me down. As I reached over to erase his message, I realized that he hadn't let me down, I'd let myself down by choosing to pursue someone who did not belong to me; and in the process, neglecting the one who did.

I had a hard time finding the exact location that I was looking for. The streets were filled, as always, with people, cars, and even horse drawn carriages. I was sidetracked for a moment, by a little boy tap dancing on top of a raggedy piece of cardboard. He looked only a little older than Jazzmine would have been, about six or seven, but he was keeping up with his brothers and had the crowd ooh'ing and aah'ing at his lightening quick feet. I smiled, bent down and placed a five-dollar bill into their collection cup and resumed my search.

I don't know why, but something made me turn and look to my left. It only took a moment for me to notice the tent with The G Spot logo sprayed across the awning. I hesitated for a moment, suddenly nervous and wondering if he would even want me here.

I took a deep breath and continued my trek. He once said that there was nothing that I could do or say to turn him away. I guess it was time to find out if what he said was true.

Verse fifty-three: that's all

"Hey, mama..." Jazzmine called.

"Yes, Pumpkin?" I answered.

"Nothing... I just wanted to say that you're cute," she giggled and ran away from me.

"You little munchkin," I laughed, and took off running behind her.

She ran behind the sofa and tried to hide behind the chair, but I could see one of her ponytails sticking up, giving away her hiding spot.

"I got you now," I announced, and reached out to hold her and give her four special kisses: one on her forehead, one on each cheek, and one on her nose.

But before my hand was able to touch her, I woke up, feeling familiar tears on my pillow. This time they weren't tears of sadness, though. They were tears of joy, and gratitude that for five wonderful years I was able to spend my life with and share my love with an angel.

"I love you, Jazzmine," I whispered. "I love you more than the stars in the sky and more than the sand on the beach."

"Same dream?" Greg asked, reaching over and wiping one of my tears away with his thumb.

"Yes," I answered and smiled through the tears. "But that's a good thing. At least I still have my baby girl in my dreams."

"And you have me and this wild sleeping young man in your bed. Now get up woman and cook us some breakfast," Greg kidded.

I beamed at my husband; loving, as usual what I saw when I looked into his eyes. Ever since the day we'd met he has never failed to make me feel like the most incredible woman in the world. Made me feel like I wanted to at least try to live up to his assessment of me.

I glanced at my two-year-old son, Gregory Adams, Jr., who'd climbed into bed between us yet again, and felt a love so strong that it nearly took my breath away.

I took a deep breath, said a quick prayer of thanks, and scooted out of bed to make my men some eggs.

Tracey's Playlist

1. *Back Down Memory Lane* ~ Minnie Rippleton
2. *It's So Hard to Say Goodbye* ~ Boys II Men
3. *Jesus Is Love* ~ The Commodores
4. *Dreamin'* ~ Vanessa Williams
5. *Every Day I Have the Blues* ~ B.B. King
6. *Little Child Running Wild* ~ Curtis Mayfield
7. *Music Is Everything* ~ Erykah Badu
8. *Baby I'm a Star* ~ Prince
9. *Heaven Help Me* ~ Deon Estus
10. *Got to Get You into My Life* ~ Earth, Wind, and Fire
11. *Baby be Mine* ~ Miki Howard
12. *All I Could Do Is Cry* ~ Etta James
13. *Ball Confusion* ~ Temptations
14. *A Child with the Blues* ~ Erykah Badu
15. *Damaged* ~ TLC
16. *Backstabbers* ~ The O'Jays
17. *Baby's Love* ~ Louisiana Purchase
18. *On My Own* ~ Patti LaBelle & Michael McDonald
19. *Dr. Feelgood* ~ Aretha Franklin

20. Breathless ~ Corinne Bailey Rae

21. You Put a Move on My Heart ~ Tamia

22. Going in Circles ~ Friends of Distinction

23. Whatever Happens ~ Vanessa Williams

24. She Works Hard for the Money ~ Donna Summer

25. After the Love Has Lost Its Shine ~ Regina Belle

26. Ladies Night ~ Kool and the Gang

27. If Only for One Night ~ Luther Vandross

28. Body and Soul ~ Anita Baker

29. The Morning After ~ Maze

30. All the Man I Need ~ Whitney Houston

31. Creepin' ~ Luther Vandross

32. Sorry Doesn't Always Make It Right ~ Diana Ross

33. A House is Not a Home ~ Luther Vandross

34. Is It a Crime ~ Sade

35. Secret Lovers ~ Atlantic Starr

36. The Other Woman - Ray Parker, Jr.

37. Dancing in The Streets ~ Martha & The Vandellas

38. Delicious ~ New Edition

39. Inside My Love ~ Minnie Ripperton

40. Congratulations ~ Vesta Williams

41. *Superstitions* ~ Stevie Wonder

42. *Don't Want to Be a Fool*

43. *Papa Was a Rolling Stone* ~ The Temptations

44. *You Made a Fool of Me* ~ Me'Shell Ndegeocello

45. *Angel of Mine* ~ Monica

46. *Tears in Heaven* ~ Eric Clapton

47. *The Tracks of My Tears* ~ The Miracles

48. *I Want You Back* ~ The Jackson Five

49. *I'm Going Down* ~ Rose Royce

50. *What Becomes of the Broken Hearted* ~ Jimmy Ruffin

51. *Don't Know Why* ~ Norah Jones

52. *We are Family* ~ Sister Sledge

53. *That's All* ~ Dianne Reeves